"When will you g... ...ar. me chief asked.

"There is still plenty of daylight left," Hototo added.

Nate had been partial to staying the night and heading out at the crack of dawn. But they had a point. It was only early afternoon. Maybe, with a little luck, he could end the grizzly's reign of terror before the day was done. "If you will have someone guide me to where the bear was last seen, I will take up its trail from there."

"I will lead you myself," Neota signed, and when his wife stiffened, he added, "Along with twenty warriors. We never go into the forest alone. Only in groups of three or more. Even that is not enough protection."

Nate gazed around the lodge. "A bear rug will look nice in here. You are welcome to Scar's hide when it is over."

"I wish I had your confidence, Grizzly Killer. But I know Scar and you do not. I have seen what he can do. By asking you here, I hope I have not made your wife a widow."

"If Scar should kill you," Hototo signed, "what do you want us to do with your body? We cannot take it to your wife. Your wooden lodge is too far."

"I do not plan to die," Nate assured him.

"No one ever does," the old warrior responded. . . .

#40
WILDERNESS
SCAR

David Thompson

LEISURE BOOKS **NEW YORK CITY**

Dedicated to Judy, Joshua and Shane.

A LEISURE BOOK®

August 2003

Dorchester Publishing Co., Inc.
276 Fifth Avenue
New York, NY 10001

ISBN 0-8439-5092-7

The name "Leisure Books" and the stylized "L" with design are trademarks of Dorchester Publishing Co., Inc.

Printed in the United States of America.

Visit us on the web at www.dorchesterpub.com.

SCAR

Historical Notes

The King Journals consist of eleven leather-bound volumes. As I have noted previously, some entries are more detailed than others. King's account of the first time he met Winona is two paragraphs long. His summary of the first rendezvous he attended ran six paragraphs. The tale you are about to read was derived from journal entries spanning nine full pages, and was remarkable not only for its length but for the effect the outcome had on Nate King.

As usual, dramatic license has been taken with the use of sign language. To replicate it throughout the story in its pure, concise form would result in a certain deceptive simplicity. For instance, to ask "Where are you going?" in sign, it would translate into "Question. You going?" "What is your name?" becomes "Question. You called?" "Where do you live?" is "Question. Where you sit?"

You see the pattern, and I feel it does not do sign justice. For the truth is, someone highly versed in sign could achieve a degree of eloquence no literal translation can match.

Now here, for your consideration, is the story of the last of the "Great Ones."

Chapter One

From the beginning he was different.

His first conscious sensation was of a warm, pleasant wetness and of something stroking his body. He liked it. From his throat issued a tiny mew, which was answered by a rumbling he would come to know extremely well. His ears also registered a licking sound and a deep wheezing. The licking he associated with the pleasant stroking. The wheezing was like his own breathing, only louder. There had to be another creature there with him, a creature that liked making him feel good. He reciprocated by poking his tiny tongue from his mouth and trying to lick whatever was licking him.

He instinctively squinted to see better, but it didn't help. The world around him was vague and dark.

The sense he relied on most was his sense of smell. He did not know a lot about himself yet, but he did know it was keener by far than any of the others.

His nose registered so many scents, he had trouble sorting them out. There was the scent of the sticky saliva on his small form, the dank scent of his home, and a rancid scent that came from beyond his range of vision. There was a sickly-sweet odor that underlay the rest. But the scent he liked the most was the pungent scent of the creature licking him. Somehow he knew that this creature was there to care for him. To protect him. In the dim recesses of his brain he recognized that it somehow was responsible for his being there. And a new sensation came over him, a feeling of deep affection and contentment.

Time passed. His knowledge expanded. He discovered that the creature he came to think of as Caregiver was gigantic compared to him. When nestled in her fur, he would glance up at her face and marvel at how high above him it was. Sometimes, when playing with his den mates, he would scamper completely around her, and it always seemed to take an eternity.

That was the other major discovery he made. He was not the only small one there. Two others shared his world, like him in every respect except they were both bigger than he was. A lot bigger. Which was why he came to think of himself as Runt.

One was a brother who loved to pounce on him and swat him about and nip at his neck with sharp teeth that hurt terribly. In his mind his brother became Mean, and would always be Mean.

The other den mate was a she, like the Caregiver. She treated him much more nicely, and would often snuggle against him when they slept. He liked playing with her, because she was never rough and never bit too hard. He always thought of her as Nice.

They played, they fed, they slept. Life was good, except for the bullying of Mean, and Runt would have been content to stay there forever. He was conscious of growing, and of hair sprouting over his body. His vision improved, but neither his eyes nor his ears could compete with the excellence of his nose. With his eyes closed, Runt could identify Caregiver and his siblings by how they smelled. Their scents, the odor of their earthen home, of the milk he relished, were all indelibly impressed on his mind.

Runt learned he had sharp teeth just like Mean. That he had four limbs, each capped with hard claws. That when Mean become too rough, it was best to place himself with his back to a dirt wall so Mean could not come at him from behind.

Fear was alien to Runt until the day Caregiver disappeared. A full belly had lulled him to sleep enfolded in the furry mantle of her body, but when he woke up he was lying in the dirt with only his den mates at his side. Lifting his head, he mewed to attract her attention. That always brought an answering grunt, but not this time. Nor did her tongue descend to wash him, as was her wont. Mewing louder, he scoured the confines of their den, but Caregiver was gone.

Panic set in. Runt rose and bleated in alarm, inciting Mean and Nice to do the same. They were shocked. They had never conceived of a time when Caregiver would not be there for them. In his anxiety he ran wildly about, frantically questing with his nose for the scent of the being who meant everything to him. Suddenly the wall seemed to open before him and he was in a part of his world he had never been in before, a part much like their den only not as high or as wide. Ahead was something new, something so remarkable he momentarily forgot about the missing Caregiver.

It was light. A circle of bright light that hurt his eyes to gaze upon it. Stopping short, he felt the hairs on his neck rise. Intuitively, he divined that the light posed a danger. That if he were to go out into it, a terrible fate would befall him. Mean brushed passed him, moving toward the brightness, and might have gone all the way had the light not abruptly been blotted out by an enormous bulk.

Caregiver had returned. She shambled past, something dangling from her mouth. As she went by, Runt caught a new scent that sent a tingle through his whole body. A liquid that was like milk and yet not like milk spattered the ground. It was red, not white. When he licked a few drops, he discovered it had a delicious taste.

David Thompson

Caregiver dropped what she was carrying, sat on her haunches, and eyed them expectantly. She grunted, as she often did when she called them to share milk. But when they rushed to her side and tried to latch their mouths to her teats, she gently nudged them toward the thing she had brought back with her.

Mean and Nice kept trying to drink milk. But not Runt. He had long understood there was a purpose to everything Caregiver did, so there must be a purpose now. Tentatively, he sniffed at the crumpled form and again inhaled the scent that had sent a tingle through him. The fur of the creature was covered with it.

The thing had four legs, but they were much thinner than his, barely more than skin and bone. It had wide eyes and ears, a long, round body, and a peculiar tail that flapped up and down when he swatted it. From its hide jutted the jagged end of a shattered bone. Its head was shorter than his and not nearly as wide, although the fact that half its face had been caved in might be to blame.

Mean and Nice were still begging Caregiver to feed them, but Caregiver refused.

Runt licked some of the red liquid. It made his mouth water and filled him with an insatiable desire for more. Greedily, he lapped at an oozing wound, and when a thick stream of the delicious red liquid gushed into his mouth, he lay and sucked at the hole as he would at Caregiver. After a while the flow stopped, and he poked at the hide with his front claws until he had made another hole. He lapped at it as he had the other, but only a few drops of red liquid trickled out.

Disappointed, Runt bit at the hide and yanked. It tore easily, exposing a pink substance underneath. Tender, pulpy matter, which he nipped at, more out of curiosity than anything else. A chunk became wedged between his teeth. Loosening it with his tongue, he inadvertently swallowed. The taste was almost as sweet and wonderful as the red liquid. He bit off another piece and this time chewed it awhile, savoring the flavor.

6

Wilderness #40: Scar

A nudge against Runt's flank brought him up on all fours. Thinking it was Mean, he turned, ready to do battle. But it was Caregiver, and she wore an expression he had never seen before. Bending, she licked him several times, as if showing how pleased she was.

The next noteworthy event in Runt's life was the day he got the best of Mean. As usual, his den brother started a fight by biting him. He protested by cuffing Mean, who tore into him with both front paws flailing.

The blows knocked Runt backward. Regaining his balance, he glared at his chronic tormentor as from deep within him boiled a fury such as he had never known. Snarling, he flung himself at Mean, driving his shoulder against his brother's and bowling Mean over. Before Mean could rise, he was on top, biting and clawing. He didn't hold back this time. Mean was his den brother, but there were limits to how much abuse he would endure.

Loud cries filled the den, cries of fright and pain. Runt was shocked to realize they were coming from Mean's throat. He was doubly shocked to see he had opened Mean's foreleg and inflicted other, slightly less serious wounds. Growling, he stepped back to await his brother's reaction.

Head hung low, Mean slowly rose. Instead of attacking, he plodded toward a corner and lay down.

Runt was surprised Caregiver hadn't intervened. She invariably did when their play got out of hand. Looking up, he saw her seated by the back wall, wearing her pleased expression. He could not say why he did it, but he walked in a circle, his head high, and uttered several loud snarls.

It was only a few sleeps afterward that their whole world changed.

A light cuff from Caregiver roused Runt from sleep. Mean was already up, yawning and grumbling. Nice sat up and looked around. They had fed not long ago, and Runt was puzzled by what Caregiver wanted.

More cuffs herded the three of them toward the bright light. Caregiver lumbered close to it, then looked back, clearly implying they should follow. But they hesitated.

They did not know what lay beyond. They would rather stay there, where they were comfortable and safe. Growling her impatience, Caregiver walked into the light and was gone.

Mean took a step, then stopped and snarled, uncertain. Nice, always more timid than either of them, hung back.

That left Runt. He, too, took a few steps, but halted. A grunt from somewhere beyond the light prodded him into advancing. Caregiver was out there, and she wanted them to join her. The light grew brighter, so brilliant he had to squint.

Amazement filled Runt at the incredible world that unfolded before him. Its immensity terrified him. He was high up on a slope. Below, for as far as could be, were greens and browns and blues, colors so vivid, so exquisitely beautiful, they made their den seem drab by comparison.

Around Runt all was white. Under his paws crunched a soft white substance a lot like dirt and yet not dirt. He sniffed at it. Some got into his nose and made him sneeze. It was cold, this white substance, but not uncomfortably so. Tentatively, he took a few steps, and suddenly the white stuff was up to his belly. He could plow through it with ease, and he liked how he sent a fine white spray flying with a swipe of a paw.

His brother and sister had emerged and were in shock.

Caregiver growled and started lower.

Mean snarled his defiance at this strange new realm and barreled after her. In his haste, he lost his footing. He tumbled and slid, ending up with his head buried in the white stuff and his butt in the air. Incensed, he came up clawing and biting at it as if it had attacked him.

Nice was her usual calm self. Placing each paw down with care, she walked by Mean without so much as a glance.

Runt was last. As the smallest, he soon became relegated to always bringing up the rear on their daily explorations. Which was fine by him. He was fascinated by this new world and loved exploring it. He liked how Caregiver often looked back to ensure he was still there until it dawned on him she was looking behind them, as if on the lookout for something that might come on them unexpected. He sensed a wariness in her that had never been there before, and it warned him this new world held dangers. He would do well to stay on his guard.

If Mean noticed Caregiver's wariness, he paid no heed. He was always straying off, always sticking his nose into things, always getting into trouble. One time he waded into water over his head and sank from view. Caregiver watched, and when he did not come back up, she plunged her head under and hauled Mean out by the scruff of his neck. Another time, he poked his nose into a hole in a large log and from it swarmed tiny buzzing things that stung his nose and mouth.

The world was filled with other creatures. Small flying things that chirped and fluttered madly away at sight of them. Large flying things that shrieked at them from on high. Small scampering things that chittered and chattered and dived into holes in the ground or dashed up trees. And large things that bounded off in fear. Nearly every living creature, Runt discovered, was deathly scared of them.

A notable exception were the Shaggies, huge, monstrous brutes, as big as his mother, with great shaggy coats and wicked curved horns. Whenever his mother wandered near them, the Shaggies snorted and stomped the ground, and Runt had no doubt they would charge if Caregiver went any closer.

What Runt liked most about his new world was the food. A smorgasbord of plenty, theirs for the taking. Leaves, twigs, roots, insects, nuts, grasses, and, of course, any creature he could catch and eat. Which was just about every one.

There were those to be wary of, though. The Shaggies, for one. Another was a type of long, slithery creature that rattled when approached, and bared long fangs. Caregiver always gave these serpents a wide berth, and Runt took that as a clue he should do the same.

Ironically, the creature that posed the greatest threat, the ones they must watch out for the most, were their own kind.

David Thompson

One day Caregiver took them to one of Runt's favorite places, the river. They had waded into the shallows and were imitating her efforts to catch fish when suddenly she snorted and splashed past them and rose onto her hind legs, something she did only when she was agitated or curious. This time she was agitated, and the growl she voiced was the loudest Runt had ever heard her utter.

The cause of her distress was a bear even larger than she, a male of their kind who stood on the opposite bank and studied them with an interest Runt found disquieting. The male wore the same look Runt did when he came on a berry patch. Instinctively, Runt moved closer to Caregiver. So did Mean and Nice. He was confident Caregiver would not let any harm befall them.

Suddenly the giant male grunted and came into the river toward them. Caregiver's increasing number of warning growls had no effect. When the male was almost halfway across, she dropped onto all fours, roared loud enough to nearly deafen Runt, and hurled herself at the interloper.

Runt was paralyzed with fright. Not for himself. For Caregiver. The male was a third again her size, with claws and teeth that dwarfed hers. But she never hesitated. She tore into the male with a ferocity that was awe-inspiring to behold. So savage was her onslaught that the male only gave a few halfhearted swings, then retreated toward the far shore. She chased him, ripping at his flanks, and didn't relent until the male had vacated the river and retreated into the woods.

Mean snorted and resumed fishing, the incident already forgotten.

But not Runt. A terrible truth had dawned. The realization that his own kind were not to be trusted. That they would kill him if given the chance. Kill him, and undoubtedly eat him. It was a sobering lesson. In all the world, the only creatures he could trust were Caregiver and his siblings. Well, Nice, anyway.

As Runt stood there in the cold water listening to the underbrush crackle to the passage of the giant male, a chill came over him that had nothing to do with the river. There and then the world lost much of its rosy luster. It wasn't the innocent playground he had imagined. It was a place where everything ate everything else. Where survival must be earned, not taken for granted.

From that day on Runt was always alert, always testing the breeze with his nose. He routinely became aware of other creatures well before Mean or Nice did, and sometimes even before Caregiver.

More time passed, and life continued to be good. They explored, they ate, they slept. Runt grew at a remarkable rate, and although Mean and Nice were still bigger, neither could match his speed or his ready grasp of new situations and experiences.

Brisk winds from the north began to blow, and the warm weather became much less so. On some of the trees, the leaves changed hue and began falling to the ground. There was a new urgency to Caregiver's feeding. She ate as if she could not get enough. And since she was feasting to excess, so did Runt and the others. Layers of fat soon cushioned them from the increasingly brisk days and frigid nights.

Then, inexplicably, Caregiver altered her diet. For days she consumed nothing but leaves and pine needles. She refused to let them eat anything else, and when Mean balked, he was roundly cuffed.

An odd lethargy crept into Runt's veins. They had not been back to the den in many suns, and he was glad when Caregiver bent her steps toward the high peaks. At last they were going home. But when they got there it wasn't the same. Once it had seemed so immense. Now there was barely room for the four of them.

Curling up close together, Runt and his family slept a sleep that seemed to know no end. Howling blasts of wind shrieked outside, but they were snug and warm. Snow mantled the peaks in deep drifts, but they slumbered on, unconcerned.

Several times over the course of their long sleep, Caregiver awoke and ventured outside. Runt always accompanied her. And always it was the same. White fluff for as far as he could see and icy air that froze his breath. He was always eager to return to the den and resume their interrupted rest.

Eventually, the sleep that seemed to have no end, had one. Runt sensed a change, a lessening of the wind, and a gradual warming. He slept fitfully. Often he got up on his own and went out to survey their snow-bound kingdom.

At last came the day when Caregiver nosed all three of them awake, a signal for them to leave their sanctuary and once again roam the outer world. Runt started to follow, but Mean growled and slashed at him. Mean had always been second and was unwilling to relinquish his position.

Rounding on his brother, Runt bared his teeth and roared. He had never done it before, and the volume of his lungs surprised even him. For a moment he thought Mean would accept the challenge and pounce, but his brother swiveled sideways in submission and bowed his head. From then on, Runt always walked right behind Caregiver. Nice came after him. Mean was now last.

Shoulder-high drifts impeded their descent, but Caregiver plowed through them as if they weren't there. In her wake she left a wide, flattened path for Runt and the others. Once below the snow line, Runt saw that the vegetation browned by winter was turning green again.

Once Runt had voided the plug formed by the pine needles and leaves he had eaten before he hibernated, he became ravenous. He couldn't stop eating. Tender shoots, roots, parts of a deer Caregiver slew. He continually crammed his gullet, and the moment each meal ended, he was hungry for more.

Time drifted by, and they enjoyed an idyllic existence.

Runt was vastly more confident, but he had learned his lessons well and never relaxed his vigilance. So it was that one warm, sunny morning, as he trudged after Caregiver toward a nearby stream, he was first to catch the scent of other bears. The odor wasn't that of his own kind but the slightly different musky scents of several black bears. Or Lesser Bears, as he tended to regard them.

Runt had encountered Lesser Bears before. Usually, when they caught a whiff of Caregiver, they wheeled and fled as fast as their paws could carry them. But not this time. For when Caregiver crested a low hill, there, waddling toward them, were a pair of Lesser Bear cubs. They were smaller than Runt, although not by much, and so absorbed in the fascinating scents and sights of the surrounding woodland that they failed to notice Caregiver until they were almost on top of her.

Caregiver growled. That should have been enough to send the cubs scurrying in flight. Instead, they threw back their heads and bawled.

Out of a nearby thicket flew the epitome of avenging motherhood.

If the mother black bear was afraid, she never showed it. If she was intimidated by Caregiver's size, she didn't let that stop her. Roaring hideously, she threw herself at Caregiver in a paroxysm of undiluted rage.

Maybe it was the suddenness of the attack. Or maybe Caregiver was distracted by the bawling cubs. Whatever the case, she was caught off guard, and before she could lift a paw to defend herself, the black bear's teeth had clamped on her neck and the black bear's claws were tearing at her body.

Runt sprang to his mother's aid. At his second bound, both she-bears broke into swirling motion. Caregiver accidentally slammed into him and he was thrown onto his back, dazed but unhurt.

Caregiver and the black bear were locked fang to fang, claw to claw. She had rallied and was giving a good account of herself, but the mother black bear was formidable in her own right and doubly so when protecting her young.

As for the cubs who had started it all, they turned to flee. Their kind were not as aggressive as Runt's. They would much rather run than fight. But they had gone only about ten strides when a smaller version of Caregiver overtook them. It was Nice. Quiet, gentle Nice, the one who never swung a paw in anger. The one who never bit too hard when at play. Only now she had been transformed into savagery incarnate. She raked one cub with her claws, spun, and sank her teeth into the other. Scarlet spurted, fueling her bloodlust, and within moments she had both cubs down and was ripping and rending first one and then the other.

Mean rushed to be in on the kill, his teeth shearing into the jugular of the smaller cub. It squalled and thrashed as its throat was ripped wide.

The mother black bear heard. She turned to dash to her offspring, and in doing so, sealed her doom. For as she turned, she exposed her own neck. In a twinkling, Caregiver's immensely powerful jaws closed at the base of her skull, and there was an immensely loud *crack*. The black bear stiffened, pawed weakly at the ground, and collapsed. Her mouth opened and closed a few times, but no sounds came out.

Runt saw all this as he rose, but he did not join his siblings. He felt no fury toward the cubs, and had no urge to kill for the mere sake of killing. His primary concern had been Caregiver, and now that she had dispatched her adversary, he watched his siblings reduce the black bear cubs to tattered slabs of pulped flesh and rent hair.

In the recesses of his mind Runt was struck by a disturbing comparison between the family of Lesser Bears and his own. Those cubs had a mother, a mother they adored as much as he adored Caregiver. And now all three were dead. Leading him to wonder if the same fate might one day befall his own family.

Nothing lived forever. It was a fact of existence. Everything died, some creatures sooner than others. Since Runt liked being alive, it seemed to him that he must devote all his energies to fending off the inevitable as long as possible. He must remember not to let his temper get the better of him, as Mean always did. Anger bred carelessness, and carelessness led to death. He must also not be prone to rash acts, as Nice had just now by impulsively attacking the other cubs. To survive, he must always keep his head in time of danger.

Runt didn't think he was hungry, but his stomach rumbled at the tantalizing aroma of fresh meat and blood. Caregiver had started to devour the mother black bear, and his siblings were each helping themselves to a cub. He did not think his mother would mind sharing, and he ambled toward her.

A sudden suggestion of movement on a slope to the south brought Runt's head up. He saw creatures winding lower through the trees. Large creatures they were, and the most bizarre he ever beheld. They had two heads and six legs as well as other limbs, and long, flowing tails. He could not tell a lot about them at that distance, but what he did distinguish was enough for him to growl a warning loud enough for his mother to hear.

Caregiver swung her great head in the direction he was gazing. The hackles on her neck rose, and she rumbled deep in her chest, a special sound reserved for when she needed them to obey without hesitation.

Nice and Mean lifted their gore-covered muzzles from their meals.

Wheeling, Caregiver headed for the nearest trees at her top speed. Runt and the others were hard-pressed to keep up, but keep up with her they did. Runt had never witnessed Caregiver behave like this. She was afraid. Caregiver, who was never scared of anything, was scared of the creatures coming down the mountain.

Whatever they were, they must be the deadliest alive.

Chapter Two

They had run a considerable distance when Caregiver halted and rose onto her rear legs to scan their back trail. Runt imitated her. Far off through the trees were the strange new creatures, and it was plain the creatures were after them. They were being hunted, just as they so often hunted other animals.

Caregiver grunted, dropped onto all fours, and headed up an adjacent slope. She traveled swiftly, silently, grimly. Her neck bled profusely from the horrible wound inflicted by the black bear, but she paid it no heed.

Mean and Nice were also silent and somber. Runt did not blame them. He sensed that they were in the greatest danger they had ever been in. Even greater than the danger from the males of their own kind.

On a bench midway up the mountain Caregiver again stopped, and wheeled. An angry snarl escaped her. The creatures were still back there, climbing swiftly. There were as many as Runt had claws on all four paws. He could see them more clearly, and what he saw bewildered him no end.

16

Wilderness #40: Scar

The creatures moved on four long lower legs but had two others midway down their bodies. A pair of smaller limbs were higher up, near the smaller of their two heads. Flowing black hair grew from the tops of both heads and at their hind ends. Their hides were a confusing mix of colors and textures. They were one color high up, another lower down. Most perplexing of all were the feathers that grew from the hair on the smaller of their heads. It had been Runt's experience that only winged creatures had feathers. But these new creatures did not have wings.

Caregiver had an urgency to her movements Runt had seldom witnessed. He noticed she appeared to be tiring. Usually she had more stamina than all of them combined, and he wondered if the loss of blood was to blame. He had seen creatures weaken quickly after being severely wounded.

Fear spiked Runt, as it had that day at the river when his mother fought the large male. Fear he might lose her. She was the single greatest thing in his existence, and he cared for her as he did no other. He watched her closely, his worry mounting as she ran at a slower and slower pace.

Finally they came to the crest of a high ridge. Here Caregiver stopped and looked down. The strange creatures were still back there, still climbing determinedly toward them. One glanced up and whooped. Others responded in kind, with much gesturing and waving of odd sticks they carried.

A knot of fury formed in Runt's chest. He wanted the strange creatures to leave them be. Rearing upright, he roared his defiance. Most animals would scurry for cover at the sound, but the creatures below yipped louder than ever and came on faster.

Runt sank back down. He looked at Caregiver and saw she was looking at him in a way she had never had. To his surprise, she came over and licked him as she had so often done when he was a cub. He licked her in return, and she placed her forehead against his and voiced a low whine such as he had never heard her make.

The moment passed, and Caregiver stepped back. Growling, she swatted at the three of them to goad them on. Mean and Nice hurried higher. Runt started to, then realized Caregiver wasn't following. Turning, he waited for her. He wasn't expecting her to do what she did—to abruptly roar and slam into him, nearly bowling him over. Her claws ripped at his flanks. In pain and shock he scrambled up and sped on up the mountain, and he didn't look back until he came to a clearing high above.

Caregiver was still where he had left her, staring up after them, her neck bright scarlet in the sunlight.

The creatures were almost to the top of the ridge. They were moving more slowly, more cautiously, but they continued to yip and howl.

Runt's fear for Caregiver eclipsed all else. He started to go back down, but something stopped him. Something internal he could not define. A sense, an intuition, a feeling he must not do so. Caregiver had driven him off for a reason, and he must do as she wanted.

Then a remarkable thing happened. The strange creatures halted and *split in half*. The upper parts broke off from the lower parts and continued on under their own power.

Runt grunted in surprise. It dawned on him that there were actually two creatures. The smaller had been riding the larger, much as baby opossums rode their mothers. The smaller had two legs, the larger had four. And now the two-legs, the ones who had feathers on their heads, were converging on his mother and making more noise than a pack of wolves, while the four-legs stayed where they were.

From that moment on, Runt always thought of them as Feather Heads. He marveled at their stupidity. As creatures went, they were puny and frail, clearly no match for Caregiver. She was many times their size and could slay any one of them with a swipe of her huge paws. He saw her face them and heard her growl, and his fear drained from him like water down a hole. She would show them. She would tear them apart if they dared match their puny might against hers. Runt didn't understand why his mother had been so fearful, or why she had driven him and his siblings off. The four of them could destroy these creatures without half trying.

The Feather Heads slunk toward her. They were not quite so noisy now, and one had advanced slightly ahead of the rest and was holding a long stick over his head.

Runt kept waiting for Caregiver to attack and send them running, but she did nothing. The strange creatures were almost to the top.

Finally, with a tremendous roar, Caregiver hurtled down the slope. It was then Runt discovered that there was more to these puny creatures than he had imagined. For as his mother charged, Feather Heads on either side of her rushed in close. Some threw long sticks they carried. Others somehow sent small feathered sticks flying from larger curved sticks. In a span of heartbeats Caregiver bristled with sticks like a porcupine with quills. They were embedded in her neck, in her chest, in her sides. Not only that, but the foremost Feather Head had stood his ground and hurled his long stick, which caught her full in the front between her tree-trunk legs, and sliced deep into her.

Caregiver halted and reared. She roared again, a roar of rage and pain, and as she stood there, her great maw agape, the Feather Heads darted in closer and unleashed another hail of sticks.

Runt was in shock. His mother's coat was splattered with red. As he looked on, a Feather Head dashed up beside her and buried a gleaming object in her body. Before the Feather Head could skip out of reach, Caregiver swung a forepaw and caught him flush across his small head and neck. Her claws sheared through his flesh as if it were soft mud, and his head went bouncing down the slope.

A collective howl rose from the throats of the Feather Heads. They swarmed around Caregiver, stabbing and thrusting. In a fury Caregiver fell on them. Within moments three were down, one with his ribs stove in, another with a limb missing, a third with half his face gone. But still the Feather Heads fought. Still they sent feathered stick after feathered stick into her giant frame. Sticks so small, it did not seem as if they could inflict much harm. Yet Caregiver was matted thick with blood, and her movements were becoming slower and slower. Her monumental reservoir of vitality was running dry.

Runt had witnessed enough. He raced down the slope to help her, whether she wanted his help or not. He had the presence of mind to use the timber and brush for cover, and he was almost there when the unthinkable occurred.

Caregiver threw back her great head and bawled like a newborn cub. Feathered shafts were jutting from her ears, from her nose, her jaw. One jutted from an eye socket. Long sticks protruded from her chest and sides. She took a few ponderous steps, then, with a loud groan, she collapsed.

The Feather Heads went wild. They howled and shrieked and pranced around her body in wild abandon.

Runt slowed to a deliberate stalk. These creatures had hurt his mother, had hurt her badly. A savage bloodlust seized him, an urge to rip them to pieces. He was about to barrel from cover when he noticed that several Feather Heads were scanning the slope for sign of him and his brother and sister. They would spot him if he broke from cover, and would warn their companions. Better, then, he wait for the right moment.

After a bit all the Feather Heads gathered around Caregiver. They were chattering like chipmunks, and several had drawn shiny objects from their hides. The same one who had thrown the long stick into the front of her chest now grabbed her under the throat and raised the shiny object as if to plunge it into her.

Runt could no longer contain himself. Venting a roar that shook the very ground, he hurtled toward them. They heard him, of course, and whirled to confront him, but by then he was in among them, his claws flashing. He upended four or five before the rest galvanized to life. A sharp pang lanced his side. Another his flank. Ignoring them, he gutted a Feather Head and left it convulsing in his wake.

They were brave, these creatures. For as Runt would bring one low, others leaped to take his place. Runt was cut, slashed, stabbed. Their long sticks sank deep into his flesh, their feathered shafts sliced through hide and muscle with deceptive ease. Ten or eleven littered the ground, yet still the Feather Heads fought with a ferocity belying their stature. Runt split one from chest to crotch, felt a sharp pang in his left side, and wheeled to find the Feather Head who had thrown the long stick into Caregiver's chest about to strike him again with a shiny object. Surging upright, Runt flung his arms wide and wrapped them around the creature's body.

The loudest howl yet was voiced by the Feather Heads as they rallied to the aid of the one in Runt's grasp. Runt was oblivious to their blows. Applying his full strength, he heard the crack and crackle of bone and saw blood spurt from the Feather Head's nostrils and mouth, and trickle from both ears.

But that was not enough to satisfy Runt. He bit down on the crown of the creature's head. His iron teeth crunched through bone into a soft, pulpy matter that was tangy to the taste but which he did not get to savor. For just then another Feather Head executed a high leap and buried a short stick with a shiny knob at one end in his face.

Torment spiked through Runt, clear down to his hindquarters. A moist, sticky sensation spread across his eyes, and a red haze enveloped the world around him. Letting go of the two-leg he had hugged to death, he tottered backward, swiping at his eyes with his forepaws. The Feather Heads pressed him, hard. His belly was pierced multiple times. So was his back. Sudden weakness came over him and he fell onto all fours.

More blows rained onto Runt's head and face. He was bleeding as profusely as his mother had been. In pure reflex he swung his powerful paws, but he missed more than he connected. It abruptly dawned on him that the Feather Heads were on the verge of doing to him as they had done to his mother.

They were killing him.

A new sound rose above the din. The sound of roars and

snarls not his own, mingled with screams and screeches from the two-legs. The downpour of blows on Runt's head and body ceased, and the next swipe of his paw across his face wiped away enough blood to reveal a sight he would never forget for as long as he lived.

Nice and Mean had come to his rescue. Bristling in unbridled ferocity, they were wreaking havoc right and left. Already, almost all the remaining Feather Heads were dead or dying, and the few who were left were fleeing in terror.

Mean went after them.

Nice finished worrying the throat of one she had slain, and came to Runt.

Only one Feather Head got away. He was the only one to reach the four-legged creatures his kind had ridden in on, and swinging up, he raced headlong down the mountain. Mean was too busy killing others to go after him. The rest of the Manes also fled, riderless, whinnying and snorting in fright.

Runt's fury faded. He had one thing, and one thing only, on his mind now. Stepping over dead Feather Heads, he crossed to Caregiver. He nudged her, but it provoked no response. Her eyes were open but vacant, her body as limp as a wet leaf. Runt nudged her again, then licked her several times. He stopped when he tasted his mother's blood in his mouth.

Nice whined like a small coyote and placed a paw on Caregiver, but there was nothing either of them could do.

Caregiver was dead.

Runt felt a new emotion, one so potent his chest felt heavy. A feeling of loss, of vast emptiness. A part of his life was gone, the part that meant the most, and which he could never reclaim.

Turning to the body of the Feather Head he had crushed, Runt examined it closely. The feathers were not part of its body, as were those of the Winged Ones, and had come loose. The hide below its neck was not its own hide but that of another animal, a Small Antler, judging by the smell, which the Feather Head had somehow attached to itself.

Runt had never encountered a creature that wore the hide of another, and he did not know what to make of it.

A sweet blood scent, like that of ripe berries, clung to the two-leg, perhaps the sweetest such scent Runt ever inhaled. Runt ran his tongue over a wound gushing scarlet and liked the taste greatly. Like the scent, the blood was sweeter than that of any other creature. He bit off a chunk of flesh and chewed. It, too, had that exceptionally sweet flavor.

Runt turned to his mother and was suddenly awash in agony such as he had never felt. Not in one part of his body but all over. Throbbing waves of pain washed through his skull as he twisted his neck from side to side to examine himself. Feathered sticks were embedded everywhere. Long sticks protruded from his sides and flanks. Not as many as were in his mother, but enough that he was losing a lot of blood and would lose a lot more before the flow stopped.

And that wasn't all. A large flap of hide from Runt's forehead kept falling across his left eye, partially obscuring his vision. Whatever that last Feather Head had struck him with had cleaved to the bone.

Runt had an urge to find a quiet, shaded spot and lie up for a spell. Formidable waves of torment were racking him, the worst spawned by a long stick stuck in his shoulder. Bending his head back as far as he could, he clamped his jaws onto it and pulled. The stick moved but did not come out all the way. He yanked again, more forcefully, and the stick slid loose with a wet sucking sound. It was drenched with blood. Biting down, he snapped it in half and cast it aside.

Nice came over. Runt lifted his head to nuzzle her, but she moved to his flank, wrapped her teeth around the end of a feathered stick, and jerked. It snapped off, leaving the tip buried inside him.

Runt stood still as his sister went from stick to stick, doing what she could to remove them. The long ones came out easily enough, but many of the short feathered variety broke off. As for his many other wounds, the cuts and slashes and stabs, there was nothing either of them could do.

A grunt reminded Runt of his brother. Mean had come back up the mountain and was next to Caregiver. His brother nosed her several times. Then he looked at each of them, wheeled, and went off into the forest.

Nice gave Caregiver a few final affectionate licks. With a last glance at Runt, she, too, walked off, but in a different direction than Mean had gone.

Runt felt a ripping sensation deep inside that had nothing to do with his wounds. His family, his precious family, was no more. Their mother had been the bond that held them together, and with her gone, an instinct none of them could deny was compelling them to go their separate ways.

Runt looked at Caregiver a final time and whined softly. Then he headed up the mountain. He knew of a stream near a secluded clearing. By sunset he had reached it, and after slaking his thirst, he sank onto his stomach with his head on his forepaws and slept. He needed rest, lots and lots of rest, but his sleep was fitful. Pain constantly woke him up. Whenever he so much as twitched, his anguish doubled.

By morning Runt was in awful shape. He felt hot all over. Not sweaty hot, as he would from the sun, but a heat that came from within his own body. Many of his wounds were festering and starting to ooze pus. He licked as many as he could reach. Then, rising, he shuffled to the stream and waded into a pool. The water rose as high as his chest. He dipped lower, immersing himself to his chin, and relished the brief relief it brought.

In the pool's surface Runt saw his reflection. He had seen it many times before, but never with a flap of hide as big as his paw hanging from his brow. Never with blood matted so thick he could not see the hair. His left cheek had been split open, and that side of his face was swollen to twice its normal size.

Runt stayed in the pool most of the day. Now and again his stomach rumbled, but he didn't go in search of food. He was too weak, and thinking of food made him queasy. He was also plagued by spells where his mind spun like a whirl-pool in river rapids. He could not take more than a few steps without it happening—added reason for him not to go anywhere.

The second night was no better than the first. Runt's whole body was aflame. His head hurt so much that merely opening and closing his eyes took all his force of will. For long intervals he lay with his chin on the ground, crushed by misery that was more than physical.

Runt thought frequently of Caregiver. Of how she had cared for him. Of how she fought off the male of their kind to save them, and how she had tried to drive off the Feather Heads and sacrificed herself for their sakes. She had been the best of mothers, and he missed her with a yearning that only grew as time went by.

Runt also thought of Nice and Mean. Each would seek a territory of their own now. Perhaps near, perhaps far. He might run into them again one day, but things would never be the same. They were his sister and brother, but the blood they shared would mean nothing. His kind were loners by nature. Except when mating, they generally stayed to themselves. And woe to another who invaded their domain.

Runt needed to find a territory, too, but it could wait until he was well enough to travel. As it was, he couldn't go more than a short distance without collapsing. His strength, his wellspring of energy, was at its lowest ebb.

Now and then Runt would also think of the Feather Heads, and when he did, his lips would involuntarily curl back from his teeth and he would growl deep in his chest. A new feeling took root. A feeling of intense and total hatred. Only one had escaped, but there might be more, and from that day on, whenever he encountered them, he would do to them as they had done to his mother and nearly done to him.

There was much about the Feather Heads Runt could not comprehend. They were so different from every other creature. So much about them was strange and alien. The feathers they wore in their hair. The hides they covered

David Thompson

themselves with. They did not have claws or talons or hooves, like most creatures, but instead had flesh-and-bone sticks at the ends of their limbs. Then there were the wooden sticks they used to hurt and slay, and the shiny objects that were as sharp as Runt's teeth. Most perplexing of all was their use of Manes to get around, rather than use of their own legs. And why was their blood and flesh so uncommonly, deliciously sweet?

The Feather Heads reminded Runt somewhat of Gluttons in that while both were small in stature, they were not afraid to confront Runt's own kind. A rare trait. Also like wolverines, the Feather Heads were extremely vicious. They hadn't simply killed Caregiver; they had slaughtered her. And they were rendered doubly dangerous by the fact that they traveled in large packs, like wolves.

Runt's world had been irrevocably changed. It was much more perilous than he ever thought. His size, his power, were not enough to ensure his survival. He must never allow the Feather Heads to catch him unawares, as they had his family. It would entail perpetual vigilance, but the alternative was to end up like Caregiver.

Morning came. Runt slowly rose and shambled to the pool. He felt worse than ever, and sinking into the cool embrace of the water did little to soothe his wounds and ease the agony. Nevertheless, he lay there until midday, at which point his empty belly insisted he go in search of food.

Runt let his nose guide him. It took him to a decayed log, which he ripped apart for grubs. From there he meandered to a marmot burrow. His nose told him the marmot was inside. Forelimbs flying, he dug down to the lowest chamber and cornered it. The marmot hissed and snarled and tried to dart past him, but a swipe of his right forelimb squashed it flat and in several greedy gulps he swallowed it down.

Runt was still famished. His nose led him along a game trail to a thicket. As he plowed into one side, a doe and a fawn shot out the other. The doe was much too fleet of hoof, but the speckled fawn was another matter. He crushed the spindly little thing before it had taken four bounds.

Wilderness #40: Scar

Runt ate slowly, savoring its soft, delectable flesh and the salty tang of its blood. He cleaned the meat from every bone and then cracked open the leg bones to get at the marrow. By the time he was done, he almost felt like his old self.

The feeling did not last long. The pain and festering sores continued to plague him for an entire cycle of the moon. Eventually, though, the pus ebbed and his wounds healed. Even the large gash on his head. From then on, for the rest of his life he would be reminded of them on wet days and cold mornings by sharp aches and stiffness.

As soon as Runt was able, he made a beeline for his mother's den and claimed it as his own. The warm days waxed and waned, and in due course the aspen leaves began to change color, a prelude to cold weather. Runt gorged in preparation for hibernation, and shortly after the first snow fell, he was curled up snug and warm, protected from the harsh elements by the only home he had ever known.

Came the spring, and Runt, like the wilderness itself, found new life and new purpose. He roved his kingdom, marking its boundaries in the traditional manner of his kind. A growth spurt increased his bulk substantially, and throughout the summer he continued to pack on muscle and sinew until by the next changing of the leaves he was as big as the male his mother fought that day long past, and still growing.

Of Mean and Nice there was no sign.

One morning, early, Runt rose from a temporary bed in a stand of firs and walked to a nearby spring to drink. He hadn't seen his reflection since the battle with the Feather Heads, so he was considerably startled by the image that stared back at him. The flap of hide had not healed properly. Part of his face was grotesquely twisted, and where there should be hair, it was bald and scarred. His split cheek had not resealed, making it appear he had three cheeks instead of two, and his one eye was slightly higher than the other.

After slaking his thirst, Runt traveled over a ridge into a valley he had never visited before. He stopped short at the sight of tendrils of smoke curling skyward from peculiar

27

conical structures beside a river far below. Scores of creatures were moving about among them, but his sight was such that he could not identify them. He needed to get closer.

Halfway down the mountain Runt bisected a frequently used trail and his nostrils were assailed by a scent he had not smelled since the day Caregiver died. Cold fury filled his veins, and he instantly veered into heavy timber and followed it down until he was close to the conical structures and those who used them as dens; the Feather Heads.

Runt had found their lair. The strange creatures were everywhere: males, females, and young ones, doing all sorts of odd things. Some males were rolling small pieces of bones. Some females were scraping at an elk hide with shiny objects. Young ones scampered and frolicked, as was the wont of the young of all kinds.

Undetected, Runt watched them, his fury growing and growing until it pervaded every fiber of his being. Until he could no longer contain it. There had to be a hundred of them, but it was of no consequence.

Throwing back his head, Runt roared his hatred and attacked.

Chapter Three

The nightmare was always the same.

In it Nate King was moving along a narrow ravine, high walls towering on either hand, when from up ahead came an ominous growl. He would raise his Hawken to his shoulder and thumb back the hammer. Then, as he rounded a bend, from out of nowhere the bear would be on him, its claws raking deep. The Hawken would go flying and he would grab for his Bowie, but the outcome was always the same; the bear bore him down and bit and slashed until he was a ravaged husk, and then it would straddle him and its mouth swoop low, and the last sensation he felt was that of his face being ripped off.

After the nightmare, Nate King always woke up with a violent start and would sit up in bed, his body caked in cold sweat, his breathing ragged, his heart pounding like the beat of a blacksmith's hammer on an anvil.

Every night it was the same. Every night for weeks on end. It got so, Nate began to question his sanity. Worse, he began to question his courage. And if there was one trait a mountain man needed more than any other, one trait essential to his survival and the survival of his family, it was courage.

Nate King lived with his Shoshone wife, Winona, and their precocious daughter, Evelyn, in a log cabin high in the central Rockies. Nate was one of a handful of trappers who stayed on after the bottom fell out of the beaver trade, and one of the first to carve a homestead from the wilderness and settle there for good.

Winona's people had adopted Nate into their tribe—which was fitting, in that Nate had adopted many of their ways as his own. He dressed in buckskins decorated with beads, Indian-style, and in his long black hair he wore an eagle feather. He wore Shoshone moccasins, not boots, and the sheath for his Bowie was adorned with rare seashells obtained in trade by the Shoshones from a tribe that lived far off near the Pacific Ocean.

Nate's Indian name, bestowed on him many years before, was Grizzly Killer. There wasn't a man alive, white or red or any mix thereof, who had slain more of the great bears than he had. His peers, his adopted people, and those of a dozen neighboring tribes considered Nate the premier grizzly killer of all time. His exploits were told and retold around many a campfire, and his reputation was such that it had spread from the Blackfeet in the northern plains to the Apaches in the arid mountains of the desert Southwest.

Nate had never bothered to count all the grizzlies he killed over the years. Not that he ever set out to be the greatest grizzly destroyer ever. Circumstance more than design led to his preeminence. He'd simply had the misfortune of coming to the Rockies at a time when the giant bears were as thick as fleas on an old coon dog, and the even worse misfortune of attracting them like a magnet attracted iron. Everywhere he went in those early days, it seemed, there was another grizzly hankering to rip him part.

But that had been long ago.

Now there were a lot fewer silvertips, and they tended to shy from humans. Nate was of the opinion that the fate of their predecessors had taught them to fear man. Which was fine by him. If he never had to kill another grizzly as long as he lived, he wouldn't complain.

But then some Utes, or Noochews as some called them, came calling. A killer griz was on the rampage. Their efforts to hunt it down and end the carnage had been in vain. So one of their leaders sought out the one man in all the mountains best suited to help them: the famous Grizzly Killer.

Any other time Nate wouldn't have minded. He was on peaceful terms with the Utes and wanted to stay that way. But unknown to them, shortly before their arrival he had tangled with a bear and been severely mauled. Not a grizzly, ironically enough. In all his run-ins with the lords of the wilderness, he had never been badly hurt. No, it was a lowly black bear that did what no griz ever could. And he had not been the same man since.

So here Nate was, on this warm and gentle summer morn, alone on the west shore of the lake near his cabin, his arms resting on his Hawken, his green eyes glumly fixed on the snowy crown of Long's Peak off to the south. Footsteps approached, but he didn't look around. He knew who it was and why she was there.

"We need to talk, husband." Winona spoke fluent English. She was a natural-born linguist, and Nate wasn't ashamed to admit she spoke his tongue better than he spoke hers.

Nate glanced at her, admiring the exquisite beauty of her finely chiseled features, and inwardly flinched as if he had been punched in the gut. "I figured as much."

"It has been three weeks since you mended. The Utes will wonder why you are taking so long."

"A few more days won't hurt," Nate responded defensively.

"That is what you said last week, and the week before." Winona placed a hand on his broad shoulder. "This is not like you. When people need help, you are always ready to do what you can. Something is bothering you, and I would like to know what it is."

David Thompson

"I'm fine," Nate said irritably, and saw her frown.

"We have been together many winters, husband. In all that time you have never lied to me, and I have always respected you for that. What has changed you? Why do you speak with two tongues to the one who loves you most?"

Nate bowed his chin in shame. His cheeks burned from her reproach, and he had to cough to clear his throat before he could respond. "Winona, I love you more today than I did the day we met," he said slowly, searching for the right words to express his innermost sentiments. She went to reply, but he held his hand up to let her know he wasn't quite done. "You're right. I fibbed. I have not been the same since the black bear jumped me."

"The nightmares still bother you?"

Nate glanced at her. "You know about them?" He hadn't said a word. It was too embarrassing.

"How could I not? Our bed is not that big." Winona smiled. "Do you remember what I told you the day you took me as your wife? Your joys are my joys. Your griefs are my griefs. In all these years we have never hid anything from each other. Please do not start now."

Nate reached up and touched a new scar just under his hairline. "I don't rightly know what's happened. I wake up every damn night so scared I can barely breathe. That damn bear did something to me, Winona, something no other animal ever has."

Winona considered his admission. "Is it the bear, husband? Or are you doing it to yourself?"

"I've lost your trail."

"Do you also have nightmares about the mountain lion?"

Nate's mind flashed back three weeks to the narrow ravine. To that horrifying interlude right after he slew the bear, when he lay helpless in a pool of his own blood. The worst thing that could happen, had happened. A mountain lion came slinking along, drawn by the scent of fresh blood. Nate would have died if not for Winona's timely appearance. "No, I don't hardly ever think about the painter, just the bear."

"Yet the mountain lion clawed you and bit you, too."

"Not that much." Nate was genuinely perplexed. The bear hurt him a lot worse than the painter. So it was natural, in his opinion, for the bear's attack to bother him more.

"I have a cousin who was prone to nightmares. They were about a war party of Bloods who raided our village and counted coup on her father and brother. Every night she relived the attack and woke up screaming."

"How does that pertain to me?" Nate was growing impatient for her to get to the point.

"So she always relived the entire raid. Every part of it. You, on the other hand, only relive part of what happened to you that day in the ravine."

Nate shrugged. "I don't see where that makes a difference. We can't control our nightmares."

"But we can worry a thing to death, and that can lead to nightmares," Winona countered. "You had never been mauled before. It has stuck in your mind, and you have made it out to be worse than it really was."

"I nearly died," Nate reminded her. "How much worse could it have been?"

Winona tenderly placed her hand on his cheek. "You have fought grizzlies and cougars galore. You have been attacked by wolves, nearly bitten by rattlesnakes, and almost gored by buffalo. Warriors from half a dozen tribes have nearly lifted your hair." She paused. "Do you have nightmares about any of that?"

"You know I don't," Nate said. "It's all part and parcel of life in the wild."

"So was the black bear attack," Winona stressed. "Yet you will not put it aside as you have done the rest. Quit thinking about it and the nightmares will stop. It's as simple as that."

Nate thoughtfully gnawed on his lower lip. She made perfect sense, but it wasn't as easy as she made it sound. He had tried to stop. Again and again he shut it from his mind; again and again it resurfaced, unbidden.

"There is something else," Winona said. "When our son

was small, he was thrown off his pony one day and sprained his ankle. Remember how he refused to ride again? How afraid he was that he would hurt himself? And do you remember what you told him?"

"The only way to conquer our fears is to face them," Nate recited. "When a man is thrown, he has to climb right back into the saddle and show life it can't lick him."

Winona grinned from ear to ear. "What was good advice for the son is good advice for the father." Rising onto her toes, she kissed him. "I have complete confidence in you, husband. You will not let this lick you, just as you have not ever let anything else lick you."

Nate was often amazed by the depth of her love. Her confidence in him was boundless, her devotion unwavering. Without her being aware, her belief in him fueled his belief in himself. Before he could stop himself, he heard his mouth say, "All right. You win. I'll pack tonight and ride out at first light." As soon as he said it, he regretted it. He'd rather wait another week or two. Maybe by then the nightmares would stop and he would be his old self once again.

Winona shocked him by saying, "You are not going alone. Blue Flower and I will accompany you."

Nate didn't want his wife and daughter to do any such thing. "I'd rather you stayed here," he said tactfully. "I don't know how long I'll be gone. It might take a while to track down this killer griz. A moon, perhaps, maybe two."

"You would have us stay here by ourselves all that time?" Winona challenged.

"I was hoping you would take Evelyn to visit Zach," Nate mentioned. Their son had a homestead in the next valley to the north, a little over a day's ride away. "Zach and Louisa are always begging us to spend more time with them."

A squeal of delight pealed from the trail that linked the lake to their cabin, as toward them streaked a pint-sized bundle of tireless energy. "Did I just hear right, Ma?" Evelyn exclaimed. "You and I are going to stay a while with Zach and Louisa?"

Winona was on the spot. She frowned at Nate, then asked

their daughter, "Would you like to do that, Blue Flower?"

"Would I!" the eleven-year-old bubbled. Clasping her hands in glee, she spun in a circle. "I love visiting them! I could sit for days and listen to Louisa talk about life in the States."

Now it was Nate who frowned. Their daughter didn't share his enthusiasm for wilderness life. So much so that ever since she was nine, she had expressed her intention of moving east once she came of age. When the time came it would tear him apart, but he wouldn't stand in her way.

"I thought we would go with your father," Winona said.

"Into Ute country?" Evelyn rejoined in disbelief. "It wasn't all that long ago, Ma, they were trying their darnedest to wipe us out. Sure, we have a truce with them. But there are still lots of Utes who don't like Pa all that much for killing some of their warriors."

Nate took advantage of the moment. "Out of the mouths of babes," he said to his wife. "You should listen to her."

Evelyn put her hands on her hips. "I'm no baby, Pa! I'll have you know I'm more than half grown."

Winona wouldn't give up. "Their leader, Neota, gave his word none of us would be harmed. I believe he spoke with a straight tongue."

"Maybe he did," Nate argued, "but Evelyn is right. If other Utes take it into their heads to get revenge for those we killed years ago, there's nothing Neota will be able to do." Indian leaders didn't wield absolute power. Any warrior, at any time, could disagree with a chief's decision and go against it.

"See, Ma?" Evelyn crowed. "Pa agrees with me. It's best if we go to Zach and Lou's."

Winona dropped the subject, but several times during the course of the afternoon and evening Nate caught her regarding him pensively. Shortly after supper, as he was cramming pemmican into a parfleche, he noticed her doing it again, and walking over, he hugged her and whispered in her ear, "Quit your fretting. It's not as if you won't ever see me again."

"In life nothing is certain," Winona philosophized. "You will need someone to watch your back."

"You can't watch me and Evelyn both. And I can't concentrate on what needs doing if I spend all my time worrying about the two of you."

Sighing, Winona rested her forehead on his chest. "My head tells me you are right, but in my heart I do not like it, husband. I do not like it one bit."

Nate glanced toward the fireplace, where Evelyn was playing with the dolls a Shoshone aunt had recently given her. Her back was to them. Bending, he kissed Winona hard on the mouth. Her tongue met his, and for breathless moments they were borne on clouds of raw passion. A giggle brought them down to earth.

"Goodness gracious, Pa. I thought you were fixing to suck ma's tongue plumb out of her mouth."

"Hush, daughter," Winona said sternly.

Nate suppressed an urge to laugh. It was rare for them to be physical in front of others, especially the children. Winona believed intimacy was best reserved for their bedroom, after everyone else was asleep. She even insisted on always "doing it" in the dark. Nate would rather have the lamp lit, but he went along with her wishes for harmony's sake.

That night, toward midnight, as Nate lay with his hands propped under his head, wondering what on earth he was letting himself in for, Winona rolled over and reached for him. Her hunger had an urgency both rewarding and disturbing. Rewarding, in that she could not get enough of him. Disturbing, in that it lent the impression she thought they were making love for the last time.

Afterward, with Winona's cheek on his shoulder and her light snores in his ear, Nate stared at the ceiling and wished there were some way to get out of going. He was under no personal obligation to the Utes. Hell, he didn't even know Neota, the chief who had paid them a visit. He was only doing it because it was the right thing to do.

If there was one creed by which Nate strove to live his

life, that was it. He remembered hearing once that Davy Crockett, the famous frontiersman who died valiantly at the Alamo, had a personal motto: "Always be sure you're right, then go ahead." It could well be Nate's own. There were times, though, instances like this, when doing what was right was the hardest thing in the world. Nate was under no illusions. It wasn't bad enough he was afflicted by chronic nightmares. He was about to ride deep into territory few whites had ever penetrated and lived to tell the tale. The Utes weren't as outright hostile as the Blackfeet or the Sioux, but they weren't fond of white incursions into their land, as their possession of quite a few white scalps attested.

Indeed, Nate's initial conflict with the Utes came about because his cabin was situated in a valley at the fringe of their territory. A valley they considered theirs. Many Utes resented his continued presence, and were not fond of the truce their leaders had agreed on as a way of repaying him for a great service he did their people.

Winona stirred, smacking her rosy lips, and Nate gazed down, his heart filled to overflowing with the feelings he had for her. He prayed to God he wasn't about to make the biggest and worst mistake of his life.

Sleep was loath to claim him, but at last it did, and for the first time in weeks Nate went the whole night without a nightmare. He awoke before first light to find his wife already up and about, making breakfast. Tugging his buckskins and moccasins on, Nate strapped his wide leather belt around his waist, aligned his Bowie on his right hip and a tomahawk on his left, then wedged a pair of flintlock pistols on either side of the buckle. A powder horn and ammunition pouch went across his chest. So did a possibles bag that hung under his right arm. Donning a round beaver hat, he stepped to the front door.

"Morning, husband," Winona said in that special husky way she always did on mornings after they had shared their bodies. "Did you sleep well?"

"Never better," Nate assured her.

"So did I," Winona said, and gave him a knowing grin. "I will have breakfast ready shortly."

"Don't overdo it. Remember, I like to eat light when I'm setting out on a long trip like this." Nate removed the bar that secured their door at night. Dawn was almost upon them, and the sky to the east had brightened a few shades. The sun would soon displace the multitude of stars sparkling in the firmament.

At that altitude mornings were invariably brisk, and this was no exception. Breathing deeply of the crisp air, Nate walked to the corral at the south end of the cabin. Their mounts and pack animals were dozing. He gathered his saddle and saddle blanket from the tack shed and soon had his big bay ready to go. He also threw a lead rope on a dependable packhorse and led it to the storage room, where he had laid out a number of items the night before. Among them were two packs, each containing a large steel trap specifically designed for grizzlies. Nate had had them custom-made years before for dealing with troublesome bears, and they had never let him down.

Nate also took an item he had made himself, a net fashioned from sturdy rope. It came in handy the time a griz kept trying to get at their horses. He had rigged it to several trees overlooking a game trail the grizzly always used, and shot the enraged brain as it struggled to break loose.

Nate had other special items, too, items he hoped he would not need to rely on. He would much rather end the grizzly's rampage with a rifle than use a trap or the net. He preferred a clean, swift kill.

Grizzlies, however, didn't always cooperate. Incredibly tough and unbelievably fierce, they were notoriously hard to die, as the mountaineers phrased it. Their thick skulls and dense layers of muscle and fat rendered them virtually bulletproof. Nate knew of cases where grizzlies had been shot fifteen to twenty times and still kept coming.

His packs loaded, Nate brought the two horses around to the front of the cabin. He tied on the parfleches containing his food and other supplies, and he was ready to go.

Going back in, Nate sat at the pine table he had crafted with his own two hands to eat the last meal his wife would make him for quite some time. His heart was heavy, but he did not let on, for their sakes.

Winona had outdone herself. She brought over a plate heaped with flapjacks ringed by scrambled duck eggs. Side dishes included steaming porridge and thin slices of fried venison. Bread rolls, butter and jam was laid before him. And to wash it all down, a pot of freshly brewed coffee.

"So much for not eating a big meal," Nate remarked.

"I'm sorry," Winona said. "I couldn't stop myself." Grinning, she crossed to the corner where their daughter was bundled in thick blankets, and gently shook them. "Rise and shine, Blue Flower. Your father is leaving soon. Have something to eat and then we will bid him goodbye."

On most mornings Evelyn was about as happy to get up as she was to do dishes. But this morning she surprised them both by bounding out of the blankets like a young antelope. Pulling on her buffalo-calf robe and raccoon-hide slippers, she padded over and pecked Nate on the cheek. "Morning, Pa." She surveyed the table and blinked. "Are we having company over and nobody told me?"

"No," Nate said, chuckling. "Your mother mistook me for a hungry wolverine, is all." His daughter's peal of laughter was music for his soul. He pulled out her chair so she could climb on, then happily listened to her chatter about everything under the heavens while shoveling food into her mouth as if she were half starved.

Moments like these, with the cabin warm and cozy and those dearest to him at his side, were those Nate cherished most. His love for them was boundless. They were literally his reason for breathing, and he couldn't envision life without them.

Some men didn't share Nate's outlook. He knew frontiersmen who would rather spend their nights drinking and playing cards than with their wives. Mountaineers who preferred to go off for long spells in the mountains rather than stay under the same roofs with their own families. To Nate's way of thinking, they were loco. They were missing out on one of life's supreme joys. A wife and children were never-ending sources of happiness. To feel Winona's arms around his neck, or Evelyn's small hand in his, always warmed his heart to overflowing.

Nate wasn't naive enough to think married life was all cream and sugar. Everyone had their bad days, and squabbles were inevitable. But the good invariably outnumbered the bad, and the best part of squabbles was patching them over.

The important thing was love. It was the cornerstone of marriage, the foundation on which every family must rest. Without it, a family wasn't a family at all. It was a get-together of strangers.

As Nate sat there sipping coffee and peering at Winona over the rim of his tin cup, he fondly recollected some of the joyous times they had shared. The births of their son and daughter. The precious years when their children were so young and adorable. The first time Zach fired a rifle and was knocked onto his backside by the recoil. That time Evelyn baked her first cake, which came out as hard as a rock and tasting like bitter roots. He had so many fond memories, so many mental treasures.

Winona usually started cleaning the table as soon as a meal was done, but this morning she sat sipping her own coffee. "I suppose I am wasting my breath. But I have to ask one last time if you would consent to us going along."

"We've been all through this," Nate said, shaking his head. As much as he would like to have them join him, their safety came before all else.

"Pa will be all right, Ma," Evelyn said brightly. "No bear can ever get the best of him, can it, Pa?"

Without thinking, Nate ran a finger over his forehead. "No bear can ever get the best of me," he mechanically repeated, and deep inside a cold wind blew.

Winona's beautiful eyes narrowed. "When a person dwells on a problem, the problem seems worse than it truly is."

"I'll keep that in mind." Unwilling to discuss it, Nate polished off the rest of his coffee in one big gulp, then rose, patting his belly. "I must have gained twenty pounds. It'll make me so tired, I'll fall sleep in the saddle."

"Just so you don't fall off," Winona said. She was smiling, being brave, but neither of them was fooled.

Nate didn't drag it out. His Hawken cradled in the crook of his left elbow, he ambled outdoors. Evelyn was suddenly quiet, and he gave her a hug and a kiss. Then came his wife's turn. Nate held her close a good long while. When he stepped back, he had a lump in his throat and his eyes were misting. Swinging onto the saddle, he made a show of gazing off toward the lake until he had regained his self-control enough to smile down at them and say, "Take care of yourselves. I'll show up at Zach's before you know it."

"We are counting on that, husband," Winona said softly.

Nate King lifted the reins and clucked to his bay—and didn't look back until he was half a mile away. They were still there, side by side, watching him. At that distance they seemed so small and frail and vulnerable, he nearly turned around. "God help me," he said aloud, and rode on into the unknown.

Chapter Four

Legend had it the Utes once lived on the plains but competition for the buffalo-rich grasslands became too fierce so the tribe migrated into the mountains and liked it so much, they stayed. The new land they chose, deep in the central Rockies, was a natural fortress ringed by craggy ramparts that discouraged outsiders.

The region contained some of the most spectacular terrain Nate King had ever seen. Mountains so high, a man had to bend his head back to see their snow-mantled crowns. Forests thick and lush. Rivers and streams wide and swift. And interwoven through it all, verdant valleys where the Utes pitched their villages. It was a literal paradise.

Nate readily understood why the Utes fought as savagely to preserve it. Ute land was *their* land and they were not overly friendly to outsiders, red or white. Consequently, despite Neota's invitation, Nate rode uneasily, the Hawken always across his thighs. He came on Ute sign now and again, but nothing recent.

Neota had left directions on how to find the river his band

was camped near at that time of year, but the landmarks were few and far between and it would be easy to stray off course if Nate had not honed his sense of direction until he was a walking compass. Whether day or night, sunshine or rain, he never became lost. Even when he did not know where he was, he always knew which direction he was traveling. And in the wilderness, that counted for more than all the maps and directions in the world.

To Nate's knowledge, no other white man had ever penetrated this far. The gorgeous scenery he beheld was being viewed by white eyes for the first time. The wonders and magnificence of the Ute homeland, like the spectacular geyser country the Shoshones claimed as their own, had to be seen to be believed.

Wildlife was abundant. Majestic bald eagles and screeching hawks soared high in the sky. The waterways teemed with fish. Herds of elk and mountain buffalo grazed unafraid in grass-rich meadows. Deer by the score roamed the woodland. Smaller game was everywhere, so that Nate could hardly turn his head without setting eyes on one kind of animal or another.

Nate breathed deep of the bracing air and felt a twinge of envy. This was the kind of country he wouldn't mind calling his own. Land as the Almighty intended it to be. As it must have been during the days of Adam and Eve in the garden.

It never ceased to amuse Nate how he once liked city life. How he had accepted the smoke and noise and congestion as normal. New York City was the largest in the States, a city so big, no other could compare. Its streets were lined with homes, businesses, and other structures crammed one against another, and perpetually clogged with people, carriages, and wagons. Silence was unknown. The babble of voices, clattering of hooves, and rattling of wheels rose in a continuous din. Even in the dead of night a man couldn't open his window and enjoy a solitary second of priceless quiet. Yet no one seemed to mind.

That was the amazing thing to Nate. Oh, some newspaper

editors occasionally took the city to task over the number of wagon accidents and the dozens of pedestrians run over each year. And now and then editorials were devoted to the harmful effects of breathing all that smoke. But nothing ever came of it.

Crime was rampant. Corruption was widespread. Graft commonplace. The people liked to joke that the only honest politicians were dead ones. Yet few cared. New Yorkers went on about their lives as if living in a cesspool were perfectly ordinary.

Nate had no right to criticize them, though. Once he had had the same outlook. He thought city life was the sum total of existence. Everything he did each day, from the time he woke up in the morning until his head hit the pillow again at night, was defined by boundaries imposed by society. He had only been as free as the politicians and the laws they made let him be. Like a horse with blinders on, he had gone about his daily routine none the wiser.

That all changed when Nate came west. The rolling vista of green prairie and emerald foothills, the majesty of the ivory-capped mountains, had taken his breath way. Never in his wildest dreams had he imagined how truly glorious they were. Those early years, he couldn't get enough. He fell into the habit of being up before first light so he could admire each breathtaking sunrise, and into sitting outside every evening to soak in the supernal beauty of each new sensational sunset. But that was only part of the change that came over him. The external part.

An inner change took place, too. Being able to live as he pleased had been a revelation. Nate could do what he wanted, when he wanted. No one was looking over his shoulder. There were no laws to abide by, no rules to follow. He wasn't accountable to anyone except his own conscience.

Nate had taken to his new life like a duckling to water. When he was younger he often daydreamed of adventure and excitement in far-off lands. Little had he realized it wasn't necessary to travel halfway around the globe. All he had to do was head for the frontier. Once across the Mississippi, every man was on his own.

A whole new realm of delights and dangers had been spread out before him, and Nate had gobbled them up as a starving man gobbles up a five-course meal.

Nate had few regrets. He was glad he had come west, glad destiny had woven Winona's skein and his into a single thread. If he had it to do all over again, he would do it pretty much as he had the first time around.

Suddenly the bay nickered and bobbed its head, returning Nate to the present. He pretended to still be adrift in thought, and without being obvious, scanned the woodland and adjacent slopes. He saw nothing to account for the bay's warning, but the horse wasn't the skittish sort. Sliding his right hand to the Hawken's breech, he curled his forefinger around the trigger and his thumb around the hammer.

Another mile brought Nate to a high pass. By then he was certain someone, or something, was shadowing him. He hadn't seen them or heard them, but he could feel their presence. And if there was one thing he had learned from his years in the high country, it was to never discount his intuition. Hunches, as the mountain men more commonly called them, had saved many a poor coon's hide. His included.

Nate took pride in his woodcraft. He had learned from the best, from old-time mountaineers like Shakespeare McNair and renowned Shoshone warriors like Touch The Clouds. When it came to stalking, and to telling when he was being stalked, he was second to none.

So it was all the more upsetting for Nate to be thwarted in his attempts to spot the party or parties responsible. He imagined they must be Utes, but they stayed remarkably well hid, even when crossing terrain where trees and brush were at a premium.

Pausing before he entered the pass, Nate gave the lower slopes a last scrutiny, then started on through. He rode twisted sideways so he could keep an eye behind him. He

David Thompson

was almost to the opposite side when a shadow rippled across the gap. It was there and it was gone. Other than a suggestion of size, Nate couldn't begin to guess what made it. Maybe a warrior on horseback. Maybe an animal. Whether man or beast, it was savvy enough not to show itself.

Riding out the far side, Nate descended a narrow trail. He hadn't gone ten yards when he drew rein, slid off, and raced back up. Crouching low, he peered into the pass, waiting for the stalker to appear. It wouldn't be long, he reasoned, but minute after minute dragged by and the pass remained empty. After a quarter of an hour it was apparent that whatever had been back there had lost interest.

Rising, Nate returned to his horses. He took his sweet time descending into the next valley and repeatedly checked behind him. Nothing appeared, though, and twilight found him traversing a bench to the southwest. Tomorrow he had one more valley to cross and he should arrive in the general vicinity of Neota's village.

At the moment Nate's priority was to find a spot to camp for the night. A knoll close to a bubbling stream was ideal. He tethered the bay and the packhorse so they could graze, filled his coffeepot with water, and hunkered in at the base of the knoll to partake of pemmican and jerked buffalo meat while waiting for the coffee to brew.

A sliver of moon rose, the signal for every coyote within earshot to yip. An owl hooted and was answered by another, and far to the northwest a lonesome wolf voiced a plaintive howl. All sounds Nate had heard hundreds of times, as much a part of the night as the stars. He sat and sipped coffee until near on to midnight. By then the fire had burned almost down to embers, and leaving it to die out, he carried his bedroll and his rifle to the top of the knoll. From there he could see well back into the trees and spot anyone, or anything, trying to sneak up on him.

Stretching out on his back, Nate propped his head in his hands and permitted himself a luxury he hadn't indulged in since leaving his homestead: He thought about Winona and

Evelyn. Invisible fingers enclosed his heart. He missed them, missed them terribly. Sadness weighed on him like the weight of the world, and he wished to God the Utes had never come to him for help.

Drowsiness set in. Nate hovered on the cusp of slumber. He was almost under when a robin twittered loudly and took noisy flight from a patch of undergrowth fifty yards distant. It snapped him awake, and his hands fell to the Hawken. Robins weren't night birds. They were active during the day. For one to make so much racket, something had to spook it.

Nate slowly sat up. A robin wouldn't be scared of a rabbit or a deer. It had to be a predator. Coyotes or bobcats weren't cause for concern, but larger meat-eaters definitely were. It might be a mountain lion, stalking the horses; painters were especially fond of horseflesh. Or it could be something a lot worse.

Breath baited, Nate raked the forest for a telltale hint. He was about convinced that whatever it was had moved on when a shadow detached itself from the surrounding darkness and moved toward the knoll. The size of the thing caused the short hairs at the nape of his neck to prickle. It was a bear.

Nate hoped it was the killer grizzly. All he needed was a clear shot and he could be on his way home as soon as he let Neota know the griz was dead. Wedging the Hawken to his shoulder, he fixed a bead on the center of the silhouette.

The bear needed to be a lot closer before Nate fired. He had to place the ball just right, either into its heart or its lungs or the brainpan. Anything less, and the bruin would be on him before he could reload. Even then, there were no guarantees. He knew of instances where bears shot through their vitals had lived long enough to rend those responsible limb from flayed limb.

The shadow stopped. On Nate's ears fell the faint but unmistakable *whoof* of a bear testing the breeze for scent. As he well knew, bears lived by their noses. Their eyesight wasn't any better than a human's, their hearing only a little sharper. By comparison, their noses were olfactory wonders. Old-timers swore that bears could smell fresh blood from a mile off when the wind was right.

One grizzled veteran of the trapping trade liked to tell of the time he was sweeping a stretch of country below him with his spyglass and he caught sight of a grizzly at least two miles west of his position. The bear kept sniffing the air while traveling purposefully eastward. Curious as to what had aroused the grizzly's interest, he kept watching. Almost a mile from where he'd spotted it, the grizzly came to a mound of brush and limbs heaped over a dead elk. A cougar's kill, most likely, but the griz helped himself.

Nate had witnessed incredible examples of grizzly prowess, too. He had learned to never take the great bears for granted, and to never, ever underestimate them. Just about the time a man thought he had grizzlies all figured out, they went and did something totally unexpected.

Now, as the giant shadow glided nearer, Nate eased back the Hawken's hammer. There was the barest of clicks. He barely heard it, and he was holding the rifle. Yet in the blink of an eye the shadow melted away. No sounds accompanied its departure. Had Nate not known better, he would have doubted the bear was ever there.

For over an hour Nate sat up, waiting. Bears were notorious for circling around to get at their intended meals from different directions. He wouldn't put it past this one to do the same. But the woods were as still as a graveyard.

At last Nate lay back down. Sleep was a long time coming. Every noise, however slight, brought him up onto his elbows. Dawn arrived much too soon. To ward off tendrils of fatigue, he made a new pot of coffee and downed three quarters of it in great gulps.

Midmorning found Nate atop a hunchbacked rise, the last of the landmarks Neota had given Winona. Below him unfolded a broad valley bisected by a river as blue as a mountain lake. Adjoining it were well over a hundred lodges arranged in traditional Ute fashion, many emblazoned with painted symbols.

Wilderness #40: Scar

Nate knew this was just one of many villages. No one knew exactly how many there were, because the Utes were so secretive. Best estimates pegged the nation as four thousand strong.

There had to be upward of three hundred in the village below. Not far from it grazed a horse herd over a thousand strong. The Utes, like many tribes, placed high value on their stock. A warrior's worth was judged not only by the number of coup he had counted but by the number of horses he owned. Wealth wasn't a concept limited to whites, although the Indian idea of riches would make most white men laugh them to scorn.

Firming his hold on the pack animal's lead rope, Nate started down. He didn't try to approach unseen. When he came to a well-worn trail he used it, and made a point to sit tall in the saddle with his shoulders thrown back and his head high. It wouldn't do for the famous Grizzly Killer to show fear.

Nate hadn't gone all that far when he heard the beat of hoofs, and around a bend up ahead appeared several young warriors. They took one look and promptly drew rein. Excited jabbering occurred, at which point they wheeled their mounts and flew back toward the village as if all the demons of the pit were chasing them.

Nate held to a walk. Reaching behind him, he opened a saddlebag and took out a special item. He imagined he would have use for it before too long, and he wasn't disappointed. The three young warriors returned with fully twenty more, several gray-haired elders at the forefront. Smiling to demonstrate his peaceable intentions, he held the object aloft.

It was a peace pipe. Exquisitely carved from hardwood and decorated with eagle feathers and the claws of a black bear, the pipe belonged to Neota. The chief had assured Winona it would ensure Nate unmolested passage across Ute land, and his unchallenged entry into Neota's village.

But the Utes confronting him now arrayed themselves

49

across the trail, four and five deep, blocking it, and an older warrior armed with a bow raised it aloft.

Nate drew rein a dozen yards away. Tucking the pipe under his belt to free his hands, he resorted to the well-nigh-universal language of tribes throughout the central mountains and across much of the plains: sign language. "Question," he asked, his fingers flowing smoothly. "Village I see Neota sit?" As was his habit, Nate mentally filled in the gaps. In English it would be. "Mind if I ask you a question? Does Neota live in the village ahead?" As languages went, sign talk was skin and bones. There were over a thousand sign symbols, but it had been Nate's experience that most tribes used only three to four hundred in their day-to-day exchanges.

The warrior with the gray hair studied Nate intently, then lowered the bow and signed, in effect, "Are you the one Neota went to find? Are you the white-eye called Grizzly Killer?"

"I am," Nate signed.

A much younger warrior with a moon face and a florid complexion moved his hands emphatically: "You finally came! Where were you twelve sleeps ago when we lost six warriors? Where were you last night?"

The old man glanced sharply at the younger and said something in the Ute tongue. The young one responded in sign, "I do not care if I offend him! My brother is dead! If this white is the fearless killer of bears we hear so much about, why did he take so long to show his hairy face?"

"I can answer that for myself," Nate signed. "I was mauled by a black bear and needed time to recover."

"Some bear killer," the younger warrior scoffed, and several other Utes smirked in agreement.

"Enough, Niwot!" the older man signed. "Grizzly Killer is here at Neota's request. You will make him welcome, as you would any honored guest."

"My brother might be alive if this white had not taken so long to get here," Niwot responded. "He has my contempt until he proves he deserves better." Reining around, the young warrior departed. Eight others went with him.

Nate had anticipated some hostility, but not this much, this soon. "I am sorry I did not arrive sooner."

The old warrior's seamed features creased in a friendly smile. "I am the one who should apologize. You must forgive Niwot. Twelve sleeps ago he lost his brother to Scar. He has been bitter ever since."

"Scar? Is that what your people call the grizzly?"

"It is more than a name. It is him. He is scarred outside and in, and from the depths of his pain our misery is born."

Nate didn't quite understand but held off asking a bunch of questions for the time being. Except for the most important. "Where is Neota? I hoped he would greet me in person."

The face of every Ute clouded, and the old warrior answered, "Scar struck again last night. He ripped open a lodge, killed the family inside, and dragged off a young woman. Neota and forty warriors went after him."

"The bear comes right into your village?" Nate once heard of a griz doing such a thing, but it had been an isolated incident. And not even that one had the undiluted gall to drag someone from their lodge.

"Scar is not like most bears, as you will learn for yourself. For now, let us conduct you to our village to await Neota's return." The old warrior stopped moving his fingers a moment. "I am called Hototo, or He Who Whistles." To demonstrate why, he whistled loud enough to be heard in Canada.

"You do that well," Nate complimented him.

"My grandfather taught me. He was a good whistler, perhaps the best our people ever had. He also taught me how to imitate bird cries." Hototo demonstrated by imitating a sparrow, a raven, and a hawk. "With my own eyes I saw him call in grouse so we could kill them to eat. And once he called in an eagle to pluck a handful of tail feathers."

It sounded far-fetched, but Nate had witnessed Crow warriors lure in eagles for the same purpose. Indians were nothing if not resourceful.

David Thompson

"You must be tired after traveling so far. Come. We will show you to Neota's lodge. He has made it known you are to stay with his family while you are with us."

Nate would much rather sleep out under the stars, but to refuse would be taken as an insult. "Lead the way."

A pall of sorrow hung over the Ute encampment. It was apparent in their bent heads and stooped shoulders. In the quiet that prevailed. And in the absence of children. Only a few women were out and about, and those who were made it a point to get to where they were going quickly. Warriors roved in pairs and in threes, armed as if for war with bows and lances and war clubs.

"The children are being kept inside," Hototo informed Nate.

"Their mothers are afraid of the bear?"

"Everyone is. Scar will sometimes attack a village two or three times in one sleep."

"But surely not in broad daylight," Nate signed. Bears did their prowling for prey at night, for the most part. Besides which, no animal in its right mind would dare confront so many humans head-on. It was unthinkable.

"Yes, in daylight, too. Scar has no fear of us. To him we are food. And, I suspect, less than food."

Nate was going to ask what the old man meant, but they came to a circle of debris and Hototo reined up.

"This is the lodge Scar destroyed last night."

The fury and force of the bear's onslaught were remarkable. The lodge had been ripped apart, claw marks in the buffalo hides leaving no doubt as to the culprit. The long poles that braced them were broken and splintered. It looked as if a tornado had struck.

"Were many killed?"

"A father and his three children. We believe the mother was slain also, but Scar dragged her off, so we cannot be sure until Neota and the search party find her." Hototo gestured. "You may have a closer look if you want."

Reining the bay over, Nate dismounted. From the look of things, the grizzly had crossed the river and scaled a nearby bank without the sentries or the camp dogs noticing. It then ripped open the rear of the lodge and burst in on the sleeping family. Nate doubted the husband had time to grab a weapon. Within seconds it had been over, and the griz had ripped its way back out again, totally destroying the lodge in the process.

"Two winters ago Scar did this to five lodges at once," Hototo glumly revealed. "He did not bother to kill all the occupants. Most he crippled by ripping off an arm or a leg. One girl, a pretty child of ten winters, had her ear bit off."

"You make it sound as if you think Scar mutilates your people on purpose," Nate signed. Which had to be one of the silliest claims he ever heard. Bears weren't vengeful. They killed to eat, and that was it.

"He does. Once Scar chewed a warrior's face half off but did not touch the rest. When the warrior healed, he could not stand to look at himself. In despair he went off into the woods to track Scar and do battle."

"And?" Nate signed when the old man did not show any indication of finishing the account.

"We never saw the warrior again. He was my oldest son."

Nate climbed on the bay, and they rode on to one of the finest lodges in the village. The hides were new, the painted symbols as bright as if painted the day before. Nate did not need to be told it belonged to someone of importance and prestige, and he could guess who.

Hototo slid off his pinto and walked to the flap. He called out in Ute and was answered by a woman. "We call her Star At Morning," he translated in sign as he stepped back. "She is Neota's woman."

The flap opened and out she came, so radiant she took Nate's breath away. Exceptionally lustrous black hair framed an oval face as smooth as marble. Full, red lips curled in greeting, showing off teeth as white as paper. Her dress was of the finest buckskin, cured to perfection and decorated with beads.

"This white man is Grizzly Killer," Hototo signed to her. Out of habit Nate doffed his hat. She looked at him quizzically, unsure what it meant. Chiding himself for being a dolt, he jammed the hat back on and signed, "My heart happy meet you."

Star At Morning's slender fingers flowed more gracefully than his ever could. "You talk sign talk good, white man."

Out of the lodge came three mirror images of their mother, the oldest not much over ten. Bashful, they clung to her dress and peeked out at Nate as if afraid he would bite their heads off.

"Fine daughters you have there," Nate signed. "Do you have sons as well?" He was making small talk. When she frowned and averted her gaze, he thought that perhaps she'd had one but lost it.

"No sons yet, Grizzly Killer, but my husband and I want one very much. Before another winter has gone by, we hope the Great Mystery will smile on our efforts."

Among some tribes boys were highly valued. So many warriors were lost to war and other mishaps, males were at a premium. So far as Nate knew, though, the Utes weren't one of them. "I wish you success and happiness. My wife and I have a son and daughter, and we love them dearly."

Star At Morning raised her hands to sign, but just as she did, from over by the river came a soul-searing shriek.

Chapter Five

A long line of weary, dust-caked warriors were filing across a ford and up the riverbank into the village. At its head rode a tall, handsome, well-proportioned warrior whose demeanor marked him as a leader.

Nate King remembered Hototo mentioning that Neota and forty warriors had gone off after the killer grizzly. Only thirty-five were returning. And the last warrior in line was leading five horses strung on a rope.

The shriek had been uttered by a woman who must be related to one of the missing men. For when the last warrior led the riderless mounts up onto solid ground, she rushed to one of the horses and clung to it, sobbing pitiably.

Neota and those with him looked like men who had been through hell and back again. As the searchers drew rein and dismounted, Utes poured from every direction. Warriors, women and children, all eager to hear what had happened. When they were all gathered, Neota began speaking. Wailing erupted, and an older woman tore at her hair and dress. Toward the end of his account, Neota raised his voice and used a lot of animated gestures.

David Thompson

Although Nate didn't understand a word, it was apparent the chief was trying to bolster their spirits. Just as it was equally apparent he was failing miserably. Every face reflected sorrow, and something else: an abiding despair. Nate saw it in their eyes, in their expressions.

The killer griz had been plaguing the Utes for years, and Nate was witnessing firsthand the emotional toll it had wrought. Neota's band wasn't the only one the bear had struck, although of late the grizzly had been focusing its attention on them more than any other.

Suddenly Nate didn't resent being there quite so much. Neota had told Winona his band was desperate, but only now did Nate have any true inkling of exactly *how* desperate they were. The people began to disperse, many of the women and children sobbing, the men as somber as cloudy days. Star At Morning was beside her husband, talking quietly.

Hototo nudged Nate. "You can talk to Neota now," he signed woodenly. The loss of the warriors had crushed the old man as it had everyone else.

Star At Morning saw Nate approach and said something to her husband. The tall Ute turned, and despite all he had been through, Neota smiled warmly and signed enthusiastically, "Grizzly Killer! My heart is glad to see you again, and gladder you have come."

"It is good to finally meet you," Nate responded. "My wife tells me I owe you my life." He had been at death's door when the Ute leader visited their cabin. The wounds inflicted by the black bear had become infected, inducing a high fever and unconsciousness that lasted days. It was Neota who helped Winona break the fever and start him on the road to recovery.

"I did as I would for any man," Neota signed.

Nate was pleased to learn the chief wasn't one of those who hated whites on general principle. "I owe you my life," he signed again, "and I always make good on my debts. I will do what I can to help put an end to this bear who has caused your people so much heartache and loss."

56

Neota gripped Nate by the shoulders and locked eyes. The emotion they conveyed said more than sign symbols ever could.

Hototo picked that moment to interject, "Grizzly Killer has just arrived. He saw Sakima's lodge." He stopped signing and added a few statements in Ute that caused Neota to straighten in anger and survey the village as if looking for someone.

"I apologize for Niwot," the chief then signed. "He is young and headstrong and has been bitter since the loss of his brother. His sentiments are those of only a small number of my people. Most are glad you are here."

"I have already forgotten it," Nate assured them. Which wasn't completely true. He would be on his guard his whole stay. There might be a few whose dislike of whites was so strong, they'd be tempted to rub him out.

Star At Morning whispered to her husband, who signed, "My wife says I have forgotten how to treat a guest. Come! I invite you into my lodge. There is much we must talk over, much we must plan."

In one of the lodges they passed, a young girl blubbered hysterically. Almost everyone except the sentries had gone inside, lending the illusion that the village was practically deserted.

Nate left the bay and his packhorse ground-hitched close to Neota's dwelling. The interior was a lot like a typical Shoshone lodge. In the center, under the air vent, crackled a small fire. Personal possessions ringed the perimeter, including everything from blankets to pans to a lance and shield.

As was customary, Nate waited until his host had sat down and beckoned before he moved to the position of honor to the left of the fire. Hototo had also been invited, and sat across from him.

While Star At Morning and her daughters busied themselves preparing food, Neota crossed his legs and bowed his head. When he looked up, he wore the same mask of despair his people had a while ago.

David Thompson

"Grizzly Killer, I will not lie to you. I will speak with a straight tongue. You can believe me when I say that unless something is done, unless Scar is killed and killed soon, my people will go the way of the Twisted River Utes."

"I have never heard of them," Nate signed.

"That is because they no longer exist." Neota shifted, making himself more comfortable. "Twenty-seven winters ago they were the most powerful Ute band of all. They occupied the Twisted River country, where game and grass were abundant. They were a happy, proud people, and other bands looked up to them and admired them greatly."

Nate settled back. The tale was going to be a long one.

"Their leader was a great warrior known in our tongue as Maska, or The Strong One. He was a good man and cared deeply for his people. He protected them as a father protects his children and saw that all their needs were met." Neota's fingers stopped a moment. "Then one day many of the young men were off hunting, Maska's son among them. They came on four grizzlies, a mother bear and three cubs."

Two cubs were average, Nate knew. The most he'd ever seen a female grizzly with was four. Three wasn't unheard of, but it was unusual.

"These young men were headstrong and brave. To prove their courage, they decided to kill as many of the bears as they could catch. They chased the four up a mountain. The she-bear turned at bay, and the warriors closed in on her."

"They were fools!" Hototo interrupted. "No seasoned warrior would be so stupid."

"As that may be, the deed was done," Neota continued. "A terrible fight took place and the she-bear was slain. The young warriors thought it a great victory. As they were about to remove her hide, one of the cubs attacked. They might have killed it had the other cubs not arrived." Neota paused again. "Only one warrior escaped with his life. Maska's son was one of those slain."

Nate was beginning to see where the story was leading.

"Many moons came and went and the she-bear and her cubs were a memory. Then one day during the Thunder

58

Moon a bear attacked Maska's village, killing and maiming. Before the warriors could rally, the bear was gone, leaving five dead and four wounded. Maska tried to track the bear but lost the sign. A council was called. All those who had seen the bear were asked to describe it so hunters would know which bear to watch for. All the witnesses said the same thing."

Hototo had been fidgeting with eagerness to join in. Now he signed, "They all said the bear was unlike any other. Not only was it huge beyond all bears ever known, but its face was wrong."

"Wrong?" Nate interjected.

"Twisted. Hairless. Scarred," Neota clarified. "So hideous, few could stand the sight. From that day on, the bear was known as Scar."

Nate was amazed. "Are you saying this same grizzly has been terrorizing your people for over two dozen winters?"

"You must think us cowards," Neota signed. "Weaklings who cannot hunt or track or kill one animal."

"No," Nate signed. Yet he couldn't help wondering how the grizzly had lasted so long. Grizzlies were tough and hard to kill—but twenty-seven *years*? "Go on with your story. The more I learn about this bear, the more I know of his habits, the easier it will be to kill him."

Hototo signed, "There will be nothing easy about killing this one."

"Maska's band went on with their lives," Neota went on. "It is rare for a bear to attack a village, and they did not think it would happen again. But it did. One moon later, in the middle of the night, Scar returned. He ripped open a lodge, as he did Sakima's lodge here last night, and slaughtered the family inside. From then on, Maska's people never knew when Scar would strike next. And strike he did. Warriors would go off to hunt and never come back. Women went for berries and were never seen again. Maska's people lived in terror, day and night."

"Did they send to other Noochew bands for help?" Nate inquired.

David Thompson

The lines in Neota's face deepened. "We Utes are a proud people. We fight our own battles. Maska would not ask others to do what he could not do himself. Over forty of his people had been killed when—"

"Forty!" Nate exclaimed aloud in English. To his knowledge there had never been a bear anywhere that had taken that many human lives. "Sorry," he signed, then thought to ask, "How many people has Scar killed altogether?"

Neota and Hototo exchanged comments, and the chief answered, "We do not know the exact number. But it would not be wrong to say it is well over one hundred."

"One hundred and fifty would be more accurate," the older warrior signed.

Nate glanced from one to the other. They were serious. Completely serious. But his mind wouldn't fit around the number. It was inconceivable. No bear could be responsible for that many human kills. To dispute them, though, would be tantamount to an insult, so he merely signed, "I would hear the rest."

"Over forty of Maska's people had been killed when he decided to leave the Twisted River country. They dismantled their lodges, packed their belongings, and loaded it all on travois. Setting out early, they passed over a ring of mountains to the north by sunset. They thought they were safe. But that night, as they slept around their fires, Scar fell on them and killed four more. They pushed on, but the next night Scar killed six."

Nate had never heard of a bear, or any other animal, waging such a relentless campaign of extermination. Because that is what it was. Scar couldn't eat six people at one time. He had done it out of bloodlust, like a rabid wolf or a painter gone berserk. *Or had he?* A troubling thought struck Nate, a thought so disturbing in its implications, he filed it away for future consideration.

"From then on, Scar struck at will. Day, night, it made no difference. Maska and his warriors did the best they could, but it wasn't enough. Only a handful were left when they reached the village of another Ute band on Spring

Creek. The other band took them in. Eighty warriors were sent into woods after Scar, but he had disappeared."

Hototo took up the account. "Several winters went by. People began to think Scar had died. That all was well. Until one night during the Grass Moon, when Scar destroyed two lodges and killed eleven people."

"It was starting all over again," Nate deduced.

"Not quite," Neota signed. "The next time Scar struck, it was at a different village, near Mesa Peak. Over a span of ten moons he was responsible for the deaths of seven more men, women, and children."

One thing had become clear to Nate. Bears were notoriously unpredictable, but Scar had to be the most unpredictable of all. Hunting the monster down would take every bit of woodlore he possessed.

"Since those long ago days, Scar has roamed at will, going from village to village. We never knew where he would strike next. We never knew when. About two moons ago, we found a pair of hunters who had been clawed to pieces. Scar's tracks were all around them. Since then, he has not left our valley. After he claimed eleven of my people, I came to see you, Grizzly Killer. Now that number is up to twenty-one."

"The five warriors you lost—?" Nate prodded.

"We tracked Scar to a mountain south of here. Halfway up we saw the woman he had carried off, lying in a clearing. We rushed to see if she was alive and made the mistake of crowding around her body. It was what Scar wanted us to do. He was on us before an arrow could be loosed. Five warriors dead, in less time than it takes me to use sign talk to tell you! Then Scar was gone, vanished into the trees, as always."

Nate had to be certain. "Are you saying you think Scar deliberately left the woman there? That he laid a trap for you and your warriors and used her as bait?"

"I do not think it," Neota responded. "I know it."

Bears weren't that canny, not in Nate's experience, anyhow. They were clever, but no more so than a fox or a cougar. The Utes would have him believe Scar was positively diabolical.

"That brings us to the present. And to you, Grizzly Killer. At Bent's Fort and elsewhere, we heard stories of your prowess. We heard how the Shoshones and the Flatheads and the Crows all regard you as the best bear slayer alive. We appeal to you for help." Neota reached out and gripped Nate's arm. "*I* appeal to you for help."

"I will not leave until the bear is dead," Nate vowed, and meant it. Whatever his personal feelings previously, they were permanently changed by the horrific account he'd just heard. Scar had to be stopped. Whether the bear's toll was as high as the Utes claimed or exaggerated was irrelevant.

"Can you kill him?" Neota bluntly signed.

"Bears are like people. No two are ever alike. Some are smarter than others. Some are stronger or faster. A hunter must adapt to each one. From what you have told me, this Scar is the most vicious bear I ever heard of. But to answer your question, yes, I believe I can."

A heartfelt smile creased the chief's countenance. "You have made me happier than I have been in many moons."

"White people have a saying," Nate signed. "Never get ahead of yourself. We must not be guilty of the same mistake. It might take a while to track Scar down. A long while." Nate tried not to think of how much he would miss his family, of how dearly he would miss holding Winona close at night.

"What do you need from us? Men to help you? I will pick fifty warriors tomorrow," Neota offered. "Do you need food? I will have my woman go from lodge to lodge, asking for salted meat and whatever else my people can spare."

"I have plenty," Nate replied. "And I prefer to work alone." Ordinarily, too many warriors in a hunting party drove all the wildlife into hiding. In Scar's case it might have the opposite effect, and lure the killer griz to him before he was ready. Neither outcome was desirable.

Hototo was regarding Nate as if he doubterd Nate's sanity. "One man alone cannot stop Scar. The best hunters in our tribe have tried. Warriors who could track a mouse through a meadow, or put an arrow through the eye of a buck at fifty paces." He clucked like an irate grouse. "Are you better than they were?"

"Certainly not," Nate signed. "I meant no offense."

"Then why do you think you can succeed where they have failed? Why are you so special?"

To avoid antagonizing the old warrior, Nate tried an indirect tack. "How many grizzlies had those hunters slain? The most by any one man?"

Hototo had to ponder a few seconds. "A warrior from the Pine Creek band had four grizzly hides in his lodge. How many have you killed?"

"I stopped counting at fourteen."

"That many?" Hototo was impressed. He turned to the chief and said in sign language, "Now I see why you were so insistent. But Scar is not like others of his kind. He is as intelligent as we are. Maybe more so. And he knows this country. Grizzly Killer does not."

"I am not afraid," Nate signed.

"You should be" was the older man's retort. "Fear will keep you alive when all else has failed you. Remember that."

Nate was spared further criticism by Star At Morning, who presented both of them with small but delicious bowls of broth. Neota and Hototo became involved in a heated discussion, and when it was over, Neota had the courtesy to translate in sign. "My friend wants to move our village down the river tomorrow. He is worried Scar will keep coming back until we do. But I think we should stay where we are. Scar might go elsewhere otherwise, and we want him to stay in the valley so you can find him and put an end to our suffering."

"I do not want anyone to die because of me," Nate objected.

"Think instead of all those who will die if Scar is not stopped. He has already slain so many. Would you have him slay more?"

"No," Nate admitted. But he still didn't like the notion of

David Thompson

Neota using his own people as an unwitting lure.

Further talk was curtailed by the arrival of more food. Star At Morning was a gracious hostess and a fine cook. Nate filled his belly to bursting with succulent venison, roasted roots that tasted a lot like potatoes, and delicious sweet cakes made from crushed berries. About halfway through the meal he excused himself and went out to the packhorse. Taking his coffeepot and coffee from a parfleche, he ducked back under the flap. "I would like to repay your kindness by sharing a pot with you," he signed after depositing them by the fire.

Hototo smacked his lips. "I have drunk the white man's mud before," he signed. "It always makes me feel ten winters younger."

Star At Morning was all too happy to fill the pot with water and set it on to boil. Soon the lodge filled with the heady aroma of percolating coffee, and Neota and Hototo breathed deep of the rare treat.

The little girls, Nate had noticed, couldn't stop peeking at him when they thought he wasn't looking. He was probably the first white man they had ever seen, and he hoped they were favorably impressed. Along about the end of the meal, as the men were contentedly sipping their coffee, Star At Morning knelt beside Neota.

"With your permission, husband, Red Sunrise would like to ask a few questions of our guest," she signed, nodding at their oldest daughter.

"If Grizzly Killer does not mind, I do not," Neota responded.

Nate smiled, "Ask all the questions you want. I have a girl about her age, so I know how they can be." Evelyn had been a bundle of curiosity since she was old enough to walk.

"My daughter would like to know why you grow so much hair on your face? Is it a white custom?" Star At Morning inquired.

"Most whites do it, but not all. I do so because shaving every day in the wild is not practical. I grew mine when I first came out here, and I have had it ever since."

"Does your wife like it?"

Now that the subject had come up, Nate couldn't recollect ever asking Winona how she felt about his beard. He'd always taken it for granted that she didn't mind. "I do not know," he admitted. Shoshones, like the Utes and most Indians in general, were clean-shaven. "But if she told me to, I would shave for her."

Red Sunrise posed another question to her mother. Neota and Hototo grinned. Star At Morning hesitated, then signed, "My daughter would like to know if all white men let their wives tell them what to do?"

Nate nearly choked on the coffee he was swallowing. He glanced at their daughter, who smiled as sweetly as could be, and put down his cup. "Many men, white and red, do not give their women any say in how their lives are lived. I do not believe in treating my wife like that. I respect her judgment and value her opinions. So I always ask her view when an important decision must be made. We are partners. Neither tells the other what to do."

Neota smiled, placed a hand on his wife's shoulder, and said something. Star At Morning translated, "My husband feels as you do, Grizzly Killer. He has always treated me with the highest respect. One of the many reasons I love him so dearly."

"We are both fortunate men," Nate signed, "to have wives so beautiful and charming." His compliment was greeted with a pink tinge in both her cheeks.

"My husband tells me your family lives in a wooden lodge near Duck Lake. Do you ever miss the company of your own kind?"

The question, Nate observed, was Star At Morning's own and not her daughter's. "I am never without white company for long. My son's wife is white. And I have a close white friend who lives several sleeps north of us." Nate refrained from telling her about the two families of white settlers who had moved into valleys south of his, since the Utes might see it as more encroachment on their territory. "Other white friends, like Blanket Chief, stop by when they are passing through." Blanket Chief was the generally accepted Indian name for Jim Bridger.

"But you and your wife like living in the mountains rather than among your own kind?" Star At Morning amended her question.

"We love being together," Nate signed, wondering what she was getting at.

"Your wife is an exceptional woman. I could not stand to live away from my people. All my relatives and dearest friends are part of our band. To leave them would crush me."

"It was not easy for Winona," Nate confirmed. "To make it up to her, we visit her people as often as we can. In the summer we sometimes stay for a moon or more."

"Why do you not live with them? Do they dislike you?"

"On the contrary. The Shoshones adopted me into their tribe. I consider them as much my people as my white friends. But I need room to live, to breathe. I need my own land on which to live."

"The land belongs to everyone. It is here for all to share."

Nate debated whether to say more. White and Indian ideas of land ownership were as different as night and day. To Indians, no one had a right to claim land as their own. "Out here that is the way. Far to the east where whites live, it is different. Whites buy and sell land as you would buy beads at Bent's Fort."

The topic turned to white customs versus Indian customs. Nate was refreshed, relaxed, and enjoying himself immensely, when Neota punctured his euphoric bubble.

"When will you go after Scar?" the chief asked, out of the blue.

"There is still plenty of daylight left," Hototo thew in.

Nate had been partial to staying the night and heading out at the crack of dawn. But they had a point. It was only early afternoon. Maybe, with a little luck, he could end the grizzly's reign of terror before the day was done. "If you will have someone guide me to where the bear was last seen, I will take up its trail from there."

"I will lead you myself," Neota signed, and when his wife stiffened, he added, "Along with twenty warriors. We never go into the forest alone. Only in groups of three or more. Even that is not enough protection."

Nate gazed around the lodge. "A bear rug will look nice in here. You are welcome to Scar's hide when it is over."

"I wish I had your confidence, Grizzly Killer. But I know Scar and you do not. I have seen what he can do. By asking you here, I hope I have not made your wife a widow."

"If Scar should kill you," Hototo signed, "what do you want us to do with your body? We cannot take it to your wife. Your wooden lodge is too far."

"I do not plan to die," Nate assured him.

"No one ever does," the old warrior responded. "We always think we will be alive to see the next dawn. But I have lived many winters, and I have learned we must always treat each day as our last, for it might well be."

"I will keep that in mind," Nate signed.

Chapter Six

Brilliant sunlight pierced the forest canopy in glittering shafts. High in the trees birds warbled and chirped. Squirrels leaped from limb to limb. Occasional butterflies flitted energetically about in the perpetual search of their kind. Bees buzzed in quest of pollen. Nate King couldn't imagine a more idyllic scene. The grim mood of the Utes seemed drastically out of place, and several times when he glanced back, he almost smiled at their tense postures and wary expressions. It was eloquent testimony to the effect Scar had on them.

Neota shared their unease. He rode with a bow in his left hand, an arrow already notched to the buffalo-sinew string.

By Nate's reckoning they were approximately four miles from the village, high on a thickly timbered slope. The chief looked at Hototo and made a few comments. The old warrior, in turn, glanced at him.

"Neota says we are near the clearing where Sakima's woman was found, and where Scar ambushed them. You will be able to pick up his tracks there."

68

Nate had already taken a good gander at the rogue bear's prints shortly after they left the village. Clearly impressed in mud along the river's edge were a perfect set of front paw prints no different from those of any other grizzly except in one regard: their size. They were some of the largest Nate ever saw.

But large or no, Nate still had confidence in his ability to bring the bear to bay. He had yet to meet a griz that could get the better of him. But he mustn't become overconfident. Cockiness led to mistakes, and could prove fatal.

Suddenly Neota reined up and pointed with his bow.

Ahead was a clearing. In the center lay the dead woman, her skin as pale as marble. Her right arm was missing, and her face partly eaten. Sprawled near her, contorted in their death throes, were the five warriors Scar had slain. Of Scar himself there was no sign.

Nate nudged his bay on, then realized no one was following him. "Are the rest of you coming?" he asked Hototo.

"No" was the frank answer. "To go closer is bad medicine. We will watch and warn you if Scar appears."

To debate the issue would be pointless, so Nate rode on. Dismounting at the clearing's edge, he looped the bay's reins and the packhorse's lead rope around a low limb. The dead warriors had been horribly savaged; two had their chests ripped open, another was missing his jaw and throat, and the last had been gutted.

Scar had left plenty of tracks in the pools of now-dry blood in which the bodies lay. One set led to the west, where crushed grass and flattened vegetation pointed Nate in the direction he must take. The hard-packed soil did not retain tracks well, but a bear Scar's size and weight could not avoid leaving ample sign.

Climbing back onto the bay, Nate reined toward Neota. "I will go on alone from here. I suggest you keep your people close to the village until this is over."

"Be careful, Grizzly Killer. Scar always watches his back trail. No one has ever taken him by surprise."

"Maybe I will be luckier than most," Nate replied, and

rode westward. The hunt had begun. He had six or seven hours of daylight left. More than enough, if Scar was like most grizzlies and had holed up until nightfall.

The spoor showed that Scar had been moving at a snail's pace. Evidently he wasn't worried the Utes would come after him, and had taken his sweet time getting wherever he was going.

Nate held to a trot, the lead rope wrapped tight around his left wrist. The bear was making his job ridiculously easy. He would overtake it in an hour or so, and pick it off from a distance. By tomorrow he would be on his way home. He couldn't believe how needlessly worried he had been, and he smiled at his foolishness.

The trail angled higher. Nate figured the grizzly must be lying low in a thicket or a gully, and he was so intent on spotting likely hiding places that he didn't keep an eye on the scrub brush on either side of him.

Suddenly the bay snorted and whinnied. Before Nate could react, a massive bulk hurtled out of the pines and slammed broadside into his mount. He had a flashing glimpse of large gleaming teeth and raking claws, and then he was thrown from the saddle and both he and the bay were tumbling pell-mell down the slope.

Nate had the presence of mind to cling to the Hawken and clasp his other arm protectively over his pistols. Cartwheeling end over end, he smashed into a sapling and winced as pain lanced from his right shoulder clear down to his toes. The sky and the earth changed places a dozen times before he came to rest with a bone-jarring halt against the charred stump of lightning-blasted tree.

Expecting the grizzly to be almost on top of him, Nate heaved to his feet and wedged the Hawken to his shoulder. But there was nothing to shoot. The slope above him was empty of all save the bay, which was struggling to stand. The packhorse was in full flight down the mountain, packs and parfleches bouncing and jiggling as if they were strapped to an earthquake.

Bewildered, Nate focused on the spot where the bear

sprang at them. It wasn't there. He searched right, he searched left. He searched high, he searched low. The griz was nowhere around.

"What the hell?" Nate blurted. He had seen the thing with his own eyes. Or glimpsed it, at least. It should have come after them after bowling the bay over, to finish what it started.

"This makes no damn sense," Nate said, and ran toward his mount. Along the way he snatched his beaver hat, which had gone flying when he tumbled and was stuck to a bush.

The bay was none the worse for the fall. Scratched a little, and bruised a little, but that was all. Nate's saddle had saved it from serious harm. Across one side were claw marks where the bear's raking paw had narrowly missed Nate's leg. The horse was quaking like an aspen leaf in a strong wind, and he patted its neck to calm it down.

Nate stepped into the stirrups. He still couldn't spot the grizzly anywhere. Inexplicably, it had run off. He hankered to go after it, but the packhorse came first. The panicked sorrel was still in full flight and wasn't likely to stop until it reached the valley floor. Reining around, he slapped his heels against the bay, sending it down the slope at a gallop.

The packhorse was courting disaster. Its lead rope was dragging and could wrap itself around a trunk or catch on something else at any moment. Which could bring the sorrel crashing down with a busted leg or two, or a broken neck.

Nate was a skilled horseman. Decades of mountain riding had honed his ability until he could hold his own with a Comanche. And the bay was the best mountain horse he ever owned. So it wasn't long before he was only a dozen yards behind the sorrel, and rapidly gaining. He kept one eye on the lead rope, which flapped and jerked like a bull-whip; twice it almost caught on trees, another time on a boulder.

As if that were not enough, several of the packs were coming loose. Nate had tied them good and tight, but they were being severely jostled, and it was a wonder any of them were still lashed on.

David Thompson

Suddenly a meadow broadened out before them, and Nate seized the moment. Slapping his legs hard against the bay, he pounded up alongside the packhorse, lunged, and seized the lead rope. Instead of trying to stop the runaway on the head of a coin, he slowly brought it to a stop.

"You lunkhead," Nate groused at the panting sorrel, although he couldn't really blame it. A charging grizzly was enough to scare the daylights out of anything.

Facing the mountain, Nate swept the higher elevations for sign of the bear. "Where the devil did you get to?" he wondered aloud.

Runt no longer thought of himself as Runt. He was no longer the smallest of his kind, but a giant among giants. Invariably, when he encountered others of his kind, he dwarfed them. In the recesses of his consciousness he was aware he had changed, and the change demanded a new way of thinking about himself.

It came to him one evening at an alpine lake. He had gone to the water to slake his thirst, and as he lowered his head, he saw his reflection. Saw his grotesquely twisted features. Saw the patch of hairless hide. Most noticeable of all were the thick ridges of bulging scar tissue that crisscrossed one another, like so many entwined snakes. There were so many, the whole left side of his face appeared to be one huge scar.

From then on, that was how he thought of himself: as Scar. It was a constant reminder of what the Feather Heads had done to him. A constant reminder of what they had done to his mother. And a reminder, not that any was needed, of what he must do to them.

At the moment, Scar lay in a thicket on a mountain slope overlooking a valley where he had found yet another Feather Head lair. And, moments earlier, a mystery that baffled him.

Scar had never relented in his campaign to wipe the Feather Heads out. He hated them as much now as he did the day they slew his mother. He had killed countless of their number, and he would go on killing them until the day he died.

Just the night before, Scar had dragged a female Feather Head from her conical den, knowing a pack of males would come after him, as they always did. He had slain five of them before the rest could flee, and then gone off to rest.

The clomp of hooves awakened him. Scar assumed the Feather Heads were hunting him, but when he crept lower, all he saw was a single two-leg and a pair of Manes. This two-leg had a strip of Wood Eater hide on its head, and instead of being bare-skinned, as was Feather Heads' wont, it had hair all over the lower half of its face.

Scar had crouched and waited, and when the Feather Head was close enough, he charged, intending to bowl the Mane it was riding over, then dispatch the Feather Head while it was down. But a startling thing happened. As he rammed into the Mane, he caught the two-legs' scent. The wind had not been blowing right for him to catch it sooner, and the instant he did, he realized a staggering fact: *This wasn't a Feather Head!*

Scar's nose was the one sense that never betrayed his trust. His eyes might deceive him at times with tricks of light and shadow. His ears were not always accurate in gauging distance and direction. But his nose never lied, never failed, never deceived. If his nose told him the creature was not a Feather Head, then the creature wasn't.

The shock caused Scar to whirl and lope off into the brush. He never liked being surprised, never liked new and strange things he could not understand. He was set in his ways, and he liked a world that was set in its ways, as well. The Feather Heads did much that he did not understand, but that was how they were. He had grown used to their strangeness.

This was different. This meant there was a new creature Scar must contend with. A creature that looked like a Feather Head and wore hides like a Feather Head, but, wonder of wonders, *wasn't* a Feather Head.

No two creatures smelled alike. No two had the same

scent, even though among the same kind of creatures, among the Shaggies and the Jumpers and the Musks and all the rest, there was a common element that identified them. A similarity in scent that set them apart from everything else.

The Feather Heads all had a certain odor about them. No two were the same, yet the commonality was there, underlying their individual odors. This new creature, this Wood Eater Head with hair on his face, had a radically different scent. It was a lot like the difference between what Scar thought of the Big Antlers and the Little Antlers.

The incident was troubling. Scar had grown to know the wilderness as well as he knew himself. He was familiar with every creature and their habits. To abruptly discover there was a creature he had never run into, and one that resembled his lifelong enemies, no less, was deeply upsetting, was deeply troubling.

Scar couldn't make up his mind what to do about it. He always killed Feather Heads without hesitation. But he bore this new creature no ill will, and he wasn't hungry at the moment. He was curious, though, intensely curious.

So it was that shortly after the new creature went flying down the mountain atop the black Mane, Scar rose and hurried after them. He could move fast when he wanted, and he moved fast now, keeping them in sight until they caught up to the smaller Mane and brought it to a stop.

Concealed in thick timber, Scar watched the new creature intently scan the higher slopes, looking for him. The creature climbed off the black Mane and spent considerable time rearranging bundles of hide on the smaller Mane's back. Scar had seen similar bundles before, in the dens of Feather Heads. Whenever he ripped them open, he found things inside. Sometimes it was food. Sometimes strange things typical of strange creatures like the Feather Heads.

Wood Eater Head, as Scar was now thinking of him, finished fiddling with the bundles and climbed on the black Mane. He squinted at the sun, glanced up the mountain once more, then turned the black Mane and rode in the direction of the Feather Head lair down in the valley.

Scar followed. He wanted to learn more about this Wood Eater Head. Learning about new creatures was an ingrained habit, for the more he knew, the fuller his belly stayed. With Feather Heads, the more he knew, the more he could kill. Whether this Wood Eater Head deserved to share their fate had yet to be established.

Scar's hump was bothering him from a feathered stick the Feather Heads shot into him earlier, at the clearing, but he gave it no more thought than he did his other wounds, both old and new.

Despite his size Scar moved as silently as a Slant Eye. The pads on his huge paws muffled the occasional crunch of a dry leaf or snap of a twig, and he was a master at avoiding low limbs and brush that might rustle against his coat.

Wood Eater Head kept looking back as if he sensed he was being shadowed, but he never spotted Scar. Scar made sure of that. Soon they reached a low slope and a game trail that wound toward the river.

Scar had used that trail the night before when he snuck down into the lair of the Feather Heads and dragged off the she. He saw Wood Eater Head study the trail, then stop the Mane and slide to the ground. Wood Eater Head knelt and picked up a brownish object. Breaking it apart, he sniffed it, then showed all his teeth, as if what he had found had made him happy.

The breeze gusted, bringing to Scar's sensitive nose an odor from the object in Wood Eater Head's paw. Surprise pulsed through him, for it was an odor he knew as well as he did that of his own body. Wood Eater Head was examining his droppings.

Scar's curiosity intensified. This new creature must be hunting him, just as the Feather Heads had done so many times. But this time he sensed something was different. There was an aspect about this new creature that was troubling, something that set it apart from the Feather Head hunters.

Scar watched as Wood Eater Head climbed back on the

David Thompson

black Mane and rode lower, following the game trail until the Mane was in close proximity to the river. There, it entered a steep-sided gully. Wood Eater Head dismounted. He removed a bundle from the smaller Mane's back, a bundle that clanked and rattled as Wood Eater Head carried it into the gully and out of sight.

Scar had never seen a Feather Head do anything like this. He wanted to go closer, but he was wary of the Manes catching his scent and alerting Wood Eater Head. Experience had taught him the two-legs had poor noses but the Manes had fairly good ones, and even better ears.

Wood Eater Head came out of the gully without the bundle. He walked to the small Mane, opened a different bundle, and took out something small, which he stuck into the deer hide on his legs. He started back into the gully, then snapped his head up and glanced into the forest.

A tingle ran through Scar. The new creature was looking almost directly at him. Somehow, Wood Eater Head sensed he was there. He held himself as still as the trees and boulders as Wood Eater Head scoured the woods around him. Wood Eater Head did not spot him. At least, Scar did not think he did, but he puzzled over why Wood Eater Head showed his teeth again, then hefted the long stick he always held, and disappeared back into the gully.

That long stick vaguely troubled Scar. It had a faint musky scent about it, like that of the Wood Eaters themselves, who lived in stick homes in the water and delighted in gnawing down trees they used in making dams. It did not have a sharp point, like the long sticks of the Feather Heads, so it must not be used to thrust and stab, as theirs were. At one end was a thick slab of wood; at the other, a hole.

Loud *clangs* rose from the gully. Scar pricked his ears, trying to fathom what Wood Eater Head was up to. He heard Wood Eater Head grunt, and a raspy sound, like that of his claws on rock. Shortly after, Wood Eater Head walked out of the gully, straight toward the trees near where Scar lay. Scar tensed, but Wood Eater Head wanted only to gather up limbfuls of leaves and pine needles. Four trips

Wood Eater Head made. Why, Scar had no idea. Presently, Wood Eater Head came backing out of the gully showing his teeth and bobbing his chin.

Wood Eater Head mounted the black Mane, stared toward the lair of the Feather Heads, then turned away from the river and headed west.

Scar was torn between his desire to see what Wood Eater Head had done in the gully and his desire to learn more about this unusual new creature. He stuck with Wood Eater Head, who roved up and down the lower slopes as if searching for something. At last they came to a broad area bare of vegetation. Riding to the center, Wood Eater Head halted and began to do the kind of things the Feather Heads did when they were settling in for the night.

Scar sank onto his belly. He had always been fascinated by how the two-legs created flame. The Feather Heads did it by rubbing two sticks together over dry grass. This new two-leg did it differently.

After gathering downed branches, Wood Eater Head squatted and opened a hide that hung across his chest. From it he took a small square of wood, which he opened. From that he took what appeared to be a piece of quartz and an unusual hard silvery twig. He also carefully removed something Scar could not quite see, and placed it on the ground beside the branches. Bending low, Wood Eater Head struck the silver twig against the quartz. To Scar's amazement, fiery sparks shot out, like those that sometimes flew from flames the Feather Heads made. Soon a tiny claw of flame blossomed. Wood Eater Head puffed on the flame until it grew and began devouring the wood.

Ever since that fateful day Scar first set eyes on the two-legs, he had marveled at their wondrous abilities. Riding the Manes, loosing feathered sticks that hurt, creating flame, there was seemingly no end. They were unique among all the creatures of the wild. And undisputably the deadliest.

Scar has seen Feather Heads kill Shaggies. He had seen them kill Large Antlers and Small Antlers. He had seen them kill Bounders. At one time or another he had seen them kill every other creature in the forest, from Winged Ones to the elusive Rock Walkers who inhabited the highest heights in the mountains. They were forever killing, killing, killing. Scar wondered if this new two-leg was the same.

Wood Eater Head filled a hollow silver stump with water from a hide and put the silver stump on a flat rock by the flame. Soon a rich, fragrant aroma filled the air, one Scar had never smelled before. He lifted his great head to try and pinpoint the source and spotted another creature that was also watching Wood Eater Head.

Well across the slope, crouched low to the ground, was a large wolf. Its gray coat blended seamlessly into the gathering twilight, rendering the lupine carnivore almost invisible. Scar had seen many wolves in his day, and they always avoided him. This one did not know he was there. It was staring hard at the Manes, and as Scar looked on, it began to slink down the slope toward the smaller one.

Oblivious to the newcomer, Wood Eater Head was rummaging in a bloated hide. Suddenly the black Mane whinnied and stomped. In a blur, Wood Eater Head whirled and snapped up the long stick with the small hole at one end. The wolf had frozen, but Wood Eater Head saw him, and the next moment a remarkable thing occurred. The long stick belched smoke and flame and made a noise like thunder, and simultaneously, a chunk of ground in front of the wolf erupted in a spray of dirt and stones.

Recoiling, the wolf spun and bolted into the trees. It didn't look back, didn't stop. Wood Eater Head slowly lowered his smoking long stick and showed his teeth yet again. He seemed to like doing that a lot. Stepping to the black Mane, Wood Eater Head stroked it and voiced soft sounds that made Scar think of the sounds Caregiver uttered when he was small.

The blast of the long stick had echoed off across the valley. Scar had never seen anything like it, and he reviewed the sequence over and over; the blast, the smoke, the eruption of dirt in front of the wolf. The three were connected, he realized. In some mysterious manner, the long stick had hurled something at the wolf, just as the bent sticks of the Feather Heads hurled feathered sticks at him.

This new long stick with the hole at one end, then, was dangerous. Perhaps more dangerous than the other sticks. Scar had to keep that in mind. His interest perked as Wood Eater Head slid a thin reed out of the long stick and up-ended a buffalo horn over one paw. Tiny black particles spilled out, which Wood Eater Head's paw poured into the small hole in the long stick. Then Wood Eater Head opened a hide that hung across his chest and took out what appeared to be a silver pebble. It, too, was shoved down the hole.

Mysteries on top of mysteries.

Scar spied on Wood Eater Head until a riot of stars dominated the heavens and Wood Eater Head had lain on his side by the flames and was nibbling on tiny pieces of dried meat.

Satisfied that Wood Eater Head wasn't going anywhere, Scar rose and headed eastward. Pangs of hunger nipped at his stomach, but he suppressed them for the time being. He wanted to check on something first. On his right a bird took violent wing, screeching in terror. Ahead, several Small Antlers caught his scent and bounded hastily away. A little later, it was a lone Long Ears that took frantic flight.

Scar's nose informed him when he was nearing the gully. He could smell the lingering scent of Wood Eater Head and the Manes. At the gully mouth Scar paused to test the breeze. Another scent registered. One he did not expect to smell. Impulsively, he entered the gully and stopped.

The air was laced with the odor of a Lesser Bear. A she, if Scar wasn't mistaken. It was most noticeable lower down, and as he shuffled forward, Scar moved his nose from side to side, a whisker above the soil. A lot of leaves and pine needles had been spread across the bottom of the gully just ahead. Scar remembered the trips Wood Eater Head had made into the forest. The odor of the Lesser Bear became stronger the closer Scar drew to the leaves and pine needles.

Why that should be was yet another mystery.

A new scent brought Scar to a stop. It was the smell of freshly dug earth. Clods of it had been scattered on both sides of the leaves and needles. Wood Eater Head had been digging. But Scar saw no sign of a hole.

Scar went to place a paw directly on top of the leaves. Suddenly the wind shifted, as it frequently did at night, and another scent, one he knew all too well, was borne to him from the river. Throwing his head back, he verified a fellow nocturnal prowler was coming up the gully toward him.

Scar turned to the right and hastened up the side of the gully. Secreting himself in high brush where he could see the bottom without being seen, he glued his eyes to a bend farther down. He did not have long to wait. Around the turn shambled the one creature in all existence that wasn't afraid of his kind, or any other animal.

Gluttons were the scourge of the mountains. Possessing voracious appetites, they never got enough to eat. Woe to the animal that crossed their path, for they would kill anything and everything with a savagery that matched Scar's own. When challenged, even by Scar's own kind, they never backed down. Yet for all their ferocity, they weren't a tenth Scar's size.

This one was barreling up the gully in customary fashion. The Glutton was almost to the leaves and needles when it caught the scents of the Lesser Bear and Wood Eater Head, and stopped. Its little nose twitching, it sniffed at the leaves and pine needles, then took a couple of steps.

Scar wasn't quite sure what occurred next. There was a loud, rending *snap*, and the Glutton vaulted into the air. It landed on its back, its body convulsing violently, and managed a short, guttural growl that ended with the Glutton going limp.

When it was obvious the Glutton was not going to get up, Scar warily padded down into the gully. Where the leaves and pine needles had been was a shallow hole. Blood coated the ground, the Glutton, and the peculiar thing that had sheared the Glutton's stout body nearly in half. A thing as hard as rock and twice as wide as Scar's front paw. A thing with serrated fangs longer and wider than his own. A thing Wood Eater Head had left there, after digging the hole and covering the thing with leaves and needles.

Gradually, it dawned on Scar that Wood Eater Head had *wanted* a creature to step on the thing. Wood Eater Head had placed it there deliberately. Scar remembered how Wood Eater Head had examined his droppings, and how, shortly after, Wood Eater Head had placed the thing in the gully.

It wasn't the Glutton Wood Eater Head had tried to hurt. It was him.

Chapter Seven

Nate King sat up late, thinking. Seated beside the crackling fire, his fourth cup of coffee cupped in his big, callused hands, he reviewed the events of the day and made plans for tomorrow. His body was bone tired, but his mind was racing like an antelope.

The hunt was under way. From now on, Nate couldn't afford to relax his vigilance, not for so much as a second. He must be fully alert every waking moment, and when he slept, he must do so with one ear primed. The tension would grate on his nerves, but it couldn't be helped.

Nate went through this every time he went after a griz. Hunting one wasn't like hunting elk or buffalo or even mountain lions. With elk and buffalo it was a simple matter of tracking them down and getting within rifle range. Mountain lions were more elusive, but once a hunter learned an individual cat's favorite haunts, picking it off was simple.

Grizzlies were another matter entirely. They were as elusive as ghosts and as wily as foxes. Getting close enough to shoot one was extremely difficult. And if they discovered they were being stalked, more often than not they would turn on the person stalking them. The hunter would become the hunted.

Nate had high hopes, though, that the hunt for Scar would soon be over. Wild animals, like humans, were creatures of habit. They settled into daily routines, from which they seldom deviated. They foraged over specific areas, slaked their thirst at certain spots. When moving about they tended to use the same trails. Nate had found the one Scar used the night before, when he dragged off the woman. Should Scar decide to pay the village another visit tonight, odds were he would use the same trail again.

The rogue would be in for an unwelcome surprise.

Nate owned two, custom-forged bear traps made from tempered steel to his specifications by a master blacksmith. Their spring-powered jaws were powerful enough to shear a ramrod in half. When they fastened onto a grizzly's leg, the bear was as good as done for. For even if it tore its leg loose, or chewed off its paw as some grizzlies had done, the loss of blood always made them easy to track and slay.

Nate was confident the trap he'd set would snare Scar if the rogue came anywhere near it. He had added an inducement the griz couldn't resist. In one of his parfleches, wrapped in an old cloth, was part of the hindquarters of the black bear that nearly killed him. As soon as he had recovered from the attack, he had gone back to the ravine to salvage what he could of the remains. Fortunately, scavengers hadn't found the body. And because it lay in a perpetually cool, shadowed cranny, putrefaction hadn't set in. Nate had skinned it and taken a lot of meat and fat back with him, along with the special part.

On the frontier nothing was ever left to go to waste. Every part of an animal was either eaten or put to some use. Indians, for instance, used buffalo hides not only in the making of their lodges, but for robes, moccasins, leggings, mittens, shirts, dresses, breechcloths, and underclothes. Bone was used to make arrowheads, dice, ladles, knives, and sewing needles.

David Thompson

Frontiersmen relied on bears for a variety of items. Bear hides were popular as rugs and robs. Bear fat was rendered into soap. Claws were worn as necklaces or used as awls. And a certain part of a she-bear was smeared on the trigger pans of traps to entice other bears into coming closer, just as beaver musk was used to lure other beaver into beaver traps.

By morning, if all went well, Scar would be caught or crippled. Nate would finish the man-killer off and light a shuck for home. He couldn't wait.

A mile or more to the north a wolf howled, the plaintive wail ululating like the cry of a lost soul. Nate wondered if it was the same wolf that tried to get at the horses earlier. He could have killed it if he were so inclined, but he chose to scare it off. He couldn't spare the time to clean and cure the hide, and he had enough pemmican and jerky to last weeks.

Not all mountaineers were so considerate. Some were downright kill-crazy. Every animal that came close was fair game for their guns, even when they had no need of meat or a new hide.

Nate had never been like that. The way he saw it, other creatures had as much right to live as he did. He never killed unless he had to. Like now. If ever there was an animal that deserved to die, Scar surely qualified. The rogue seemed intent on wiping the Utes from the face of the earth.

Suddenly the night was rent by another sound, a tremendous, sustained roar that filled the valley from end to end. It came from the direction of the gully. Grabbing his rifle, Nate leaped to his feet. It had to be Scar! The griz was caught in the trap and venting its pain and rage. But as he listened more closely, a kernel of doubt took root. He had heard grizzlies roar before, and this roar wasn't so much one of pain as it was defiance and challenge. He tried telling himself he was imagining things, but as he sat back down and poured himself another cup of coffee, he couldn't shake a nagging feeling that something had gone wrong.

Nate stayed up another hour in the hope of hearing Scar

roar again or make some other sound, but in vain. At last he leaned back on the parfleches serving as his pillow, pulled a blanket to his chin, and closed his eyes. The Hawken lay beside him, and his pistols were still wedged under his wide leather belt. He placed a hand on each, then tried to drift asleep. But rest was denied him.

It had been years since Nate last hunted a griz, and he had forgotten how his mind would constantly race. He'd forgotten how sharp his senses became and how his nerves were always on edge.

The prospect of imminent death always made a person feel a thousand times more alive. At any second the bear might come rushing out of the darkness. Nate scanned the bare slope he had deliberately chosen for his camp but saw no cause for concern. Closing his eyes, he tried to relax.

Nate reminded himself that nothing could get close without the horses alerting him. But it was small comfort. Grizzlies were incredibly swift. Faster than a man running flat out, faster than a horse at full gallop. Were Scar to rush him, the horses' whinny might come too late. The rogue would reach him before he squeezed off a shot.

For another hour or better Nate tossed and turned. Finally his weary body refused to be denied and he drifted to sleep despite himself. He dreamed he was stumbling through a forest as black as pitch. His footsteps were unnaturally loud, his breathing was like the wheeze of a bellows. He was afraid, deathly afraid. Something was stalking him. He couldn't see it or hear it, but it was there nonetheless. On he stumbled, bumping into trees and boulders everywhere he turned and praying for a glimmer of light that never came. Then, after an eternity, he heard a sound behind him. He turned, and out of the darkness swooped a gigantic mouth rimmed with teeth as long as sabers. He tried to cry out, but the giant maw snapped shut, and his last sensation was of his body being cleaved in two.

With a start Nate sat up. He was caked with sweat and his heart was thumping as if he had run ten miles. His throat felt parched, and when he tried to swallow his mouth was as dry as sand. He pulled his hands from under the blanket and was horrified to see them shaking. He tried to stop it and couldn't.

The last thing Nate needed was for his nightmares to return. Throwing the blanket off, he poured a cup of cold coffee and raised it in trembling fingers to his lips. He drank in gulps, feeling slightly better with each swallow. The tremors passed, but he was deeply troubled. The hunt had hardly started and he was a wreck. He couldn't battle the bear and his own mind, both. It wouldn't do. It wouldn't do at all.

Nate yawned, and was surprised to detect a brightening of the eastern sky. Dawn wasn't far off. He had slept longer than he thought, but nowhere near enough. He still felt tired, drained, and his day was only beginning.

Picking up a stick, Nate poked in the charred remains of the fire until he uncovered a tiny glowing ember. A handful of dry weeds sufficed to rekindle a flame, and soon he had fresh coffee perking. A couple of hot cups and several pieces of pemmican later, and he felt invigorated enough to saddle the bay and load the packs on the sorrel.

As a golden crown lent regal elegance to the horizon, Nate rode eastward. Most hunters would be anxious to reach the gully and learn whether Scar had been caught in the trap, but he held the bay to a walk. The truth was, lingering anxiety, courtesy of his nightmare, had formed a knot of dread deep in his gut. He wasn't the least bit eager to get there. Quite the contrary.

Eventually, Nate came around a bend in the trail and there it was, mired in shadow, its mouth gaping like the teeth-rimmed maw in his nightmare. Nate drew rein. He had to get control of himself. He was acting like a child, not a grown man. Dismounting, he tied the bay and the sorrel to a pine, pressed the Hawken to his shoulder, and slowly advanced. He had only gone a few yards when the sight of fresh bear tracks brought him to a stop. They overlaid his own from the evening before. Scar had been there, all right.

Firming his grip on the rifle, Nate edged nearer. If Scar had been caught in the trap, then he might still be there.

The stake was solid iron, and Nate had yet to see the bear that could pull it out of the ground. The links were as big around as his wrist, much too thick for a griz to bite through or snap.

The temperature was in the fifties, but to Nate it felt a lot colder. Another step, and he was in the gully. It took a few seconds for his eyes to adjust, and when they did, even longer for him to make sense of what he was seeing. His special custom-made trap was gone. The leaves and pine needles he had covered it with were churned and scattered, and where the trap should be was the slumped body of an animal a lot smaller than a bear. Its back was to him, and Nate couldn't quite identify it.

Confused, Nate inched forward. He nudged it with the toe of his left moccasin and it flopped over. Instinctively, he leaped back, and came within a hair of squeezing the trigger. For of all the animals in the wild, the kind lying at his feet were as universally feared as grizzlies. It was a wolverine. Or, rather, *half* a wolverine—specifically, the upper half. The lower half was nowhere around.

Bending, Nate saw shreds of fur and stringy bits of flesh dangling from the severed waist. The serrated pattern was typical of his trap. Apparently, the wolverine had blundered into it before Scar came along. But where was the rest of the wolverine? And what had happened to the trap?

Bear tracks lined the right-hand slope. Turning, Nate cautiously went up it. The sun was high enough now, the gully was awash in light. So was the lower half of the wolverine, on its back at the top, a puddle of blood staining the earth under it. A little farther on was the trap. Or what was left of it.

Nate raked the woods for sign of Scar before venturing closer. He had a feeling the bear was long gone, but he wasn't taking chances.

The trap had cost Nate more than five ordinary beaver traps combined. The blacksmith who made it assured him nothing short of a keg of black powder could destroy it. Yet here it was, wrecked beyond repair. Both the upper and lower bows were bent, the base twisted, the dog crumpled like so much paper. Sliding his left hand through the metal loop at the end of the anchor chain, Nate carried the trap over to the packhorse. Although it was useless, the steel could be reused.

The sorrel snorted and shied at the scent of the wolverine blood, and Nate had to grab the lead rope to keep it from rearing. Removing a pack, he put the trap inside and quickly tied the flap shut again to smother the odor.

What next? was the question uppermost on Nate's mind. He had counted on his traps to bring a swift end to the hunt. But now that Scar was familiar with them, snaring the man-killer would be that much harder.

Forking leather, Nate rode to the top of the gully and took up Scar's trails where it entered the woods. The griz had headed straight on up the mountain at a sustained lope, rare for a bear unless it was after prey. He reckoned Scar had a ten- to twelve-hour lead. Overtaking him would take most of the day.

Images of Winona and Evelyn briefly filled Nate's thoughts. He missed them more than ever, and it didn't help his peace of mind any that it could well be weeks before he saw them again.

Nate began racking his brain for a means of killing Scar sooner rather than later. Steel traps were well and dandy, but he had slain a lot of grizzlies long before he owned one. He should do as he had done in the old days, and rely on his wits and his woodcraft.

By noon Nate was above the tree line. Scar's tracks skirted a talus slope and paralleled a ridge leading southwest. From there they climbed a short slope to a narrow ravine. Nate immediately drew rein. Horrific memories of the mauling knifed through him. Once again he felt the black bear's teeth slicing into his flesh. Once again he winced to the slash of powerful claws.

Nate stared into the ravine's shadowed depths. No way in hell was he going in, not even if he knew for sure Scar was in there. Clucking to the bay, he wheeled and rode back a dozen yards to a cluster of boulders. Roosting on one about waist-high, he munched on jerky while mulling his options.

There was a very good chance Scar would return to the ravine along about sunset. Nate could set the second trap, but in light of the condition of the first, he might end up losing both and have nothing to show for it.

Approximately eight feet to Nate's right, where the ground started to slope down the other side of the mountain, stood a rock slab half the size of his family's log cabin. Biting into another tangy piece of jerky, he led the horses over and hid them behind it, out of sight of the ravine.

Nate flattened and snaked around to where he had a clear shot. Folding his arms, he rested his chin on his wrist and settled down to wait. Of all the virtues a hunter possessed, patience was the most valuable. Being a competent tracker was of benefit. So was the ability to put a lead ball through a fist-sized target at fifty paces. But neither benefited a hunter much if he lacked the patience to follow spoor from one end of the earth to the other, or to lie in wait for hours on end for his quarry to show itself.

Nate had always prided himself in that regard. When he was younger, he could wait motionless from sunrise until sunset if he had to. But it had been years since he had been called on to do so; years since his hunting skills had been taxed to any great degree. Without realizing it, his skills had atrophied. He had grown soft around the edges, and was no longer the man he had once been.

That became evident two hours after Nate took up his post. His shoulders and knees took to hurting, and his nerves to sizzling like bacon in a frying pan. He could hardly stand to lie still. Repeatedly, he resisted an urge to rise and stretch his legs.

Nate blamed married life. Or, to be more exact, what he had let married life do to him. He had it too easy. Three delicious meals a day, every day. A down bed to sleep in at night, every night. A roof over his head to keep him warm and safe. Abundant game for the table, often a stone's throw from his doorstep.

Nate's life had become as soft as a city dweller's, and he had paid the same price a city dweller paid. It had long been his opinion that civilization dulled the mind and turned hard muscle to flab. He had seen it happen many times. Former mountain men who left the high country for the lowland took to eating too much and drinking too much and idling away their time on a tavern stool or in a rocking chair. Men who could once climb the highest peaks without breathing hard couldn't climb a flight of stairs without huffing and puffing.

Nate wasn't quite that bad off, but he was far from satisfied with his performance so far. The nightmares had a lot to do with it, but not all. He needed to buckle down. He needed to toughen his mind and body, particularly the former. Otherwise, he might as well mount up and head home like a licked cur with its tail between its legs. And that he would never do. Call it pride. Call it stubbornness. He had never given up in his life, and he would be damned if he would start now.

The itching faded. His nerves quieted. Nate lay as still as the rock slab as its shadow crawled toward the ravine. His stomach growled off and on, then stopped entirely. He grew drowsy but fought it off.

Sunset was a spectacular rainbow of vivid hues, a blazing tapestry no seamstress could copy. Mars appeared, the prelude to more stars winking bright. And still Nate lay in wait for Scar. Gradually the sky darkened, the wind intensified. It had to be two hours after sundown when Nate reluctantly conceded that the grizzly wasn't going to show.

Stiffly rising, Nate stretched to relieve a kink in his lower back and stomped his moccasins to alleviate cramps in his calves and thighs. His long wait had been for nothing. Scar had gone on out the other side of the ravine and must be miles from the valley. In the morning, Nate would work his way around to the other side of the mountain and take up the trail. At the moment he needed to find a spot to pitch camp, preferably somewhere with water and grass for the horses.

Descending a mountain in the dark wasn't for the timid. A single misstep could prove costly. Consequently, it took Nate twice as long to go down as it had to go up. He'd about resigned himself to going clear down to the river when a vagrant gust of wind set the bay to nickering and bobbing its head as it always did when water was nearby. He gave the horse its head and within minutes had reined up in a verdant glade nurtured by a spring.

Mechanically, Nate went through the motions of stripping the bay and the sorrel. He gathered wood, got a fire going, and put coffee on. Disappointment ate at him like acid. He couldn't delude himself any longer. The hunt was going to take a lot longer than he wanted. He thought of Winona and grit his teeth.

Damn that grizzly, anyhow.

Once, long ago, a large group of Feather Heads gave chase after Scar attacked their lair. There were too many for Scar to fight, so he tried to shake them off his trail, without success. They were persistent.

Scar was able to keep ahead of them, though. He had learned that while Manes were fast on flat, open ground, they did not do as well in heavy timber, and were slower than newborn fawns on steep slopes. So he led the Feather Heads straight up a mountain. Several times they had to climb off their Manes and lead them, it was so steep.

Still, Scar realized they were not going to give up. Eventually they would catch him. He could not run forever. But he could make a stand. So when he came to a gorge, he hurried into its shadowed depths and crouched behind some large boulders.

In due course the Feather Heads followed him in. The gorge was so narrow, they had to ride in single file, exactly as Scar foresaw. He waited until they were almost on top of him, then tore into them with his claws flying. They fought desperately. But in the narrow confines they could not exploit their greater numbers. Singly and in pairs they opposed Scar, and singly and in pairs they died. Only a few made it out alive.

Scar had learned an important lesson, one he never forgot, one he tried to use again this day to kill Wood Eater Head. The hairy-faced hunter was only one creature, but Scar had seen what the creature's strange thunder stick could do. And just as he knew he should avoid a rabid wolf or a she-bear with cubs, so he knew, too, that the thunder stick was capable of doing him great harm, perhaps even inflicting a fatal wound. He must not let the Wood Eater Head use it against him.

Scar had noticed how the Wood Eater Head spent the night on a slope barren of plant growth, and how when riding the black Mane, the Wood Eater Head always stuck to open ground. The strange two-leg was deliberately avoiding heavy brush and closed-in spaces, which hinted to Scar that the two-leg, and his thunder stick, had a weakness.

After leaving the gully where Wood Eater Head had placed the object that killed the wolverine, Scar headed straight up the mountain to a ravine near the crest. He had been there before. There were many turns and twists, many boulders to conceal him. He would let the two-leg get close, then spring before the two-leg could resort to the thunder stick.

But Wood Eater Head never entered the ravine.

Scar waited and waited, and when the sky grew dark and gave birth to stars, he crept to the entrance in time to see Wood Eater Head ride from behind a large slab of rock and head down the mountain. Wood Eater Head had waited all day for him to come out. The creature was as patient as he was clever.

Silently padding to the rim, Scar watched Wood Eater Head descend. He considered attacking, but there was a lot of open ground between them and there was the thunder stick to consider. He was also famished. He hadn't eaten the night before and needed to remedy his oversight.

Turning, Scar traveled eastward to a tract of sparse firs

and on down into the forest proper. He stopped frequently to raise his nose into the wind. Midway to the valley he was electrified by the scent of a herd of Large Antlers. Careful to stay downwind, he circled the meadow they were grazing in until he spied a calf.

The herd was clustered together out toward the center. Scar needed them to venture closer before he committed himself so he could strike quickly before they ran off or one of the big bulls challenged him. The bulls were as tall as he was and weighed almost as much, and their long antlers were as formidable as his claws.

Unaware of his presence, the herd came slowly nearer. Scar stood as if formed from stone, anticipating his meal. A few drops of saliva dripped from his lower jaw.

The Large Antlers were now so close, Scar heard the chomp of their teeth and saw them flick their ears. The calf and her mother were not yet near enough, but soon would be. Older shes, those with more experience, had their calves in toward the middle of the herd where the males could better protect them.

Scar saw a male lift its head and start toward the young mother. He could wait no longer. Exploding from cover, he roared as he charged. It had the desired effect of freezing the calf in place. Four bounds and Scar was there. Too late, the calf galvanized to life. Scar clamped his jaws on its neck and whirled as several males rushed toward him. He reached the trees before they could intercept him, and they did not follow him in.

The calf kicked a few times and was still. Scar carried it a goodly distance, to a spine overlooking the river, and sank down to gorge in peace. Ripping off great chunks of hide to expose the tender flesh underneath, he ate with relish. His gaze drifted to the Feather Head lair, off across the valley. Starlight bathed their conical dens. From the tops of most wafted columns of smoke.

Scar had been so busy dealing with Wood Eater Head, he had not given any thought to the reason he was there to begin with.

Tearing off a large chunk of meat, Scar chewed with little enthusiasm. He must never forget what the Feather Heads had done to Caregiver. Thinking of his mother made his heart heavy in his chest, as it always did. To this day he could still see her in his mind's eye, as vividly as if she were standing right beside him. He relived, yet again, those terrible moments when the Feather Heads slew her, and by the time he was done eating, an old, familiar feeling had come over him. A feeling his insides were on fire. There was no resisting the urge that compelled him to rise and pad to the river. He forded it at a different spot than the last time, and concealed himself in a stand of cottonwoods.

Almost all the Feather Heads were in their dens, as was their custom after the sun went down. Several were over by the Mane herd, making noises together. He watched as one came toward the cones. Recognition flickered. It was the same two-leg who had led the Feather Heads to the clearing that day. He saw the two-leg stoop, push a hide aside, and enter a cone.

Lowering his head, Scar charged. He heard barking to his left and a shout from the Feather Heads near the Manes. He rapidly gained speed, hurtling past several intervening cones. From one stepped a Feather Head, who yelped and ducked back in. Scar let him go. He was solely interested in the leader of the pack. More shouts and screams pierced the night, and the leader poked his head out. He saw Scar.

Running flat out, Scar slammed into the cone with the force of a dozen stampeding Shaggies. His claws split the hide as if it were a long-rotten liver and suddenly he was inside. The leader of the Feather Heads leaped at him, wielding a long stick, but a swat of Scar's forepaw sent the puny two-leg flying. Over against the other side crouched a she and several cubs. In a twinkling Scar was on them. The she reared and stabbed a sharp silver stick into his shoulder, then whirled to scoop up her cubs and run. Scar bit down on her head and felt her skull split apart. The cubs wailed like coyotes. He dispatched all three with a swipe of his paw, and he was out of the cone and racing for the river before the Feather Heads could rally and try to stop him. He made it across unhindered and looked back.

Bedlam had seized the Feather Heads' lair. Feather Heads were running every which way, the females and young shrieking, the males bellowing in fury.

Pleased with himself, Scar loped off into the night.

Chapter Eight

Nate King was enjoying the first good sleep he'd had in days when distant noises invaded the comfortable mental cocoon in which he was wrapped. Sluggishly struggling up through a misty veil, he lay listening to faint screams and shouts and wondered if he was awake or dreaming. Then it hit him where the noises were coming from, and he shoved his blanket off and stood.

Trees blocked much of the valley floor from view. Nate moved to other side of the glade but still couldn't see the village. He did not hear war whoops mingled with the others' cries, which told him the village wasn't under attack from a hostile war party. It had to be something else.

It had to be Scar.

Nate started toward the bay but thought better of saddling up. He was too far off to be of help. It would take him a couple of hours to get there, and by then the rogue would either be dead or long gone. He was better off waiting until daylight.

Sitting back down, Nate shook the lukewarm coffeepot

to gauge how much was left, and poured half a cup. Leave it to the damn griz to spoil his rest. He should turn back in, but he was fully awake and would only lie there twiddling his thumbs.

Taking a sip, Nate leaned back on his parfleche pillow and contemplated how best to put an end to Scar's rampage. So far the man-killer had made a fool of him. He had to think of a way to lure it in close enough for a clear shot. With some bears, hanging a buck carcass near trails they frequented did the trick. But he doubted Scar would fall for so plain a ploy.

Nate had to admit old Hototo had been right about one thing. Scar *was* different from other grizzlies. He was more fierce, more brazen, more intelligent. Exactly how intelligent was hard to say, but Nate suspected the deformed brute might be the most deviously cunning griz he had ever gone up against.

From time to time there appeared certain animals that broke the mold in which their kind was cast. Animals that defied explanation. Animals endowed with almost human intellect.

Nate recollected a tale told by Jim Bridger about a wolf that plagued the early trappers. Instead of avoiding humans like most wolves, this one had gone out of its way to make the trappers' lives miserable. It had raided their traps and taken prized beaver. It ran off or killed their horses. It destroyed their supplies. Bridger and his friends tried everything they could think of to slay it, but nothing worked. The lupine demon always outwitted them. Then, one day, by a sheer fluke Bridger returned to camp early and saw the wolf tearing apart their packs. He made a spectacular shot, one he said he could never repeat if his life depended on it, and ended the wolf's inexplicable rampage.

Scar was a lot like that wolf. The death of his mother had launched him on a vendetta the likes of which was unheard of in the annals of the Rockies. Killer bears cropped up now and again. Grizzlies and black bears sometimes developed cravings for human flesh, and hunted humans as they did other game. But none could hold a candle to Scar. If what the Utes had told Nate was true, Scar was in a class by himself. His campaign went beyond hunger. Raw, unbridled vengeance drove him. A bloodlust that would never be satiated this side of the grave.

There had to be a way to stop him, Nate mused. Finding it was the challenge. He thought about some of the other grizzlies he had slain, and how he had gone about it, in the hope of hitting on a method that would work with Scar. Bit by bit drowsiness set in, and Nate was no closer to a solution when he drifted off.

How long he slept, Nate was unsure. Suddenly a sound penetrated his slumber, and he opened his eyes to find a gigantic shape looming over him. He grabbed for his pistols, but the grizzly's mouth clamped onto his right arm and he was shaken like a child's rag doll. His arm snapped like a dry twig and blood spurted over his face and neck. "No!" he screamed, clutching at his Bowie. He had to live! He had to hold Winona in his arms again, and hear Evelyn's hearty laugh. As the Bowie slid clear, the bear's teeth sheared into his face. Nate threw himself backward and felt his skin rip. He thrust blindly at the furry form above him but couldn't drive the grizzly off. Then a paw streaked out of nowhere, catching him on the side of his head, and he was sucked into a whirlpool from which there was no return.

Nate's eyes snapped opened and he sat up. Perspiration soaked his buckskins, and his heart hammered in his ears. He'd had another nightmare. Wiping a sleeve across his face, he exhaled in relief. It had seemed so real, he could still feel the bear's teeth tearing at his flesh.

"Damn me, anyhow!" Nate exlaimed. A check of the sky showed dawn was an hour off. Rather than try and get back to sleep, Nate got the fire going. The light and the warmth were welcome. So were the two cups of scalding hot coffee he treated himself to.

Shortly thereafter Nate was in the saddle and making for the river. He forded it above the village, which he reached just before sunrise. He heard wailing long before he saw the women in mourning or the four blanket-covered bodies laid in a row near what was left of a lodge. A warrior was on his knees in front of the bodies. The rest of the tribe stood at a respectful distance, sorrow hanging over them like a cloud.

What with the predawn gloom, and the fact that the warriors' back was to him as he rode up, Nate failed to recognize who it was until he dismounted. The jolt was like a physical blow. "No!" he breathed in dismay.

Hototo materialized beside him, as downcast as everyone else. "Star At Morning and her three daughters are no more," he signed.

"Question. More killed?"

"Only them," the old warrior responded, and nodded at the grieving husband and father. "He has been like that for a long time now, but no one wants to disturb him."

Neota was bent over the blanket covering his wife, her bloody hand clasped in both of his. His hair was loose and had spilled over his face, hiding his features. His shoulders were moving up and down, but he made no sound.

Nate was flabbergasted. Of all the lodges in the village, how was it that Scar had selected theirs? It had to be coincidence. The grizzly couldn't possibly know Neota was the one who had requested his help in bringing the reign of terror to an end.

"We will commit them to the next world when the sun has risen," Hototo revealed. "To the third heaven where all Utes go."

"Has anyone gone after the bear?" Nate inquired.

"No," Hototo tiredly signed. "Scar has done what no other enemy ever could. He has broken our spirit. We will spend the day in mourning and tomorrow move our village to a valley far to the north."

"That will not end the killing. Scar will follow you."

Hototo frowned and replied, "What else would you have us do? Stay here and live in dread?"

"So long as you are here, Scar will stay in this area. And I will have a better chance of finding him and killing him."

David Thompson

"It has been two sleeps since you left us," Hototo noted, "yet Scar still lives and our people yet suffer."

The suggestion that Nate should have already disposed of the grizzly bothered him. Did the Utes think he was some kind of miracle worker? he wondered. He was set to point out that it was hardly fair to blame him for the deaths of Star At Morning and the girls, when Neota rose, looked around, and strode purposefully toward them.

"You have come at the right time, Grizzly Killer. When the sun is overhead, you and I will ride out together after the slayer of my family."

The last thing Nate needed was to be partnered up with someone whose turbulent emotional state might get them both turned into maggot bait. But how could he tell that to Neota? The answer: He couldn't. Luckily, Hototo unwittingly spoke up for him.

"Is that wise, Neota? You are too upset to think clearly. Would you have Scar kill you as he has your loved ones?"

"More than I have ever wanted anything, I want him to try," Neota signed.

"You would throw your life away."

"Without my wife and daughters it has no meaning," the Ute leader responded. "I will gladly embrace death. But not until I have justice for their loss. Not until Scar is no more."

Hototo glanced at Nate, his expression saying as plain as any sign language that they must not let Neota go through with it. But what could Nate do? "I will wait by the river," he signed, and led his animals off.

A formal ceremony was held on behalf of the departed, but Nate did not attend. No one had invited him. Many tribes did not permit outsiders to witness the disposal of their dead. The Apaches went so far as to always conduct their ceremonies in the middle of the night.

Nate had been surprised to learn, on first coming west, that while some tribes buried their dead, just like whites, many more did not. The deceased were hoisted onto raised platforms and left there for the elements to whittle on until there was nothing left but bones and tattered clothes. Or they were placed in crannies up in the rocks and covered with brush and stones. Or, in a few tribes, they were burned.

Nate sat at the water's edge and listened to the beat of drums and the chants of the mourners. The whites had no name for this river, just as much of Ute territory was unmapped and unnamed. In that respect the Utes were more fortunate than other tribes. The Shoshones and Crows were not pleased that the white man had overrun their lands in search of prime beaver plews, and even less happy that almost all the beaver, as well as the mountain buffalo the whites relied on heavily for food, had nearly been wiped out.

Nate's friend and mentor, Shakespeare McNair, was of the opinion that one day hordes of whites would swarm west of the Mississippi River to claim the prairie and the mountains as their own. When Nate scoffed, McNair reminded him of all the eastern tribes who had been displaced or exterminated.

"Our kind always want to know what is over the next hill, and to lay claim to it once we find out what's there," McNair had said. "We like to explore, but we like to conquer even more. We'll never rest until we have the whole world at our feet."

Nate hoped his friend was wrong. He loved the mountains and the prairies, and loved even more the freedom that came from being able to live as he pleased. If more whites came flocking in, they'd bring with them their laws and politicians, and the wilderness would go all to hell. It would be the end of not only his way of life but of genuine freedom itself.

West of the Mississippi the only sovereign power was a man's sovereign will. His freedom was absolute. Until someone experienced it, they couldn't truly comprehend how wonderful it felt. Gone were society's shackles. Absent were the dictates of a thousand and one petty laws.

Nate could no more forsake his freedom than he would give up life itself.

David Thompson

A bustle of activity was taking place in the village. Some of the Utes were moving in solemn procession toward a hill to the west. Not all were going, and among those who had stayed behind was one who was striding toward the river, and Nate. It was the young hothead, Niwot, who couldn't be much over sixteen, if that.

Rising, Nate greeted him with a curtly signed "What do you want?"

"Perhaps you do not know, but I was with Neota when he visited your wooden lodge," the youth replied.

Nate knew, all right. Winona had related every detail of their visit. Including the young warrior's interest in their daughter.

"I would like for you to give this to Blue Flower," Niwot signed, and sliding his right hand up under his left sleeve, he removed a bracelet of blue beads. "I made this for her as a token of my pledge to court her when she is old enough."

Nate checked an impulse to slug the upstart in the face. He had to remind himself that whites' ways were not Indians' ways, and that by some tribal standards Evelyn would soon be of marrying age. "I thought you were mad at me over the death of your brother?"

"What does that have to do with taking your daughter as my wife?" Niwot rebutted. "I want her, not you."

Nate's right fist involuntarily clenched, but he willed his fingers to uncurl. "My daughter is too young for marriage."

"Now she is," Niwot signed, "but in three or four winters she will be old enough. I will ask her then to come live with me."

"You have it all planned out."

"She is pretty, your daughter, and worthy of her Shoshone name. She will grow into a fine woman any man would be proud of." Niwot gazed to the northeast. "She is smart, too, that one. I can see it in her eyes. She speaks the white tongue and the Shoshone tongue, and in the short while we were at your lodge, she learned some of our tongue, too."

Wilderness #40: Scar

Was Nate hearing correctly? Niwot admired Evelyn for her intelligence? "Do us both a favor and pick a Ute girl."

"My mind is made up, Grizzly Killer. Give this to her." Niwot wagged the bracelet.

The young warrior's arrogance was galling. "Give it to her yourself," Nate signed roughly, "when she is old enough to have suitors."

Niwot, surprisingly, did not become angry. "How old will that be?"

"Sixteen winters," Nate signed. "Five winters from now." He was confident the young Ute wouldn't wait that long. And even if Niwot did show up, Evelyn might be gone. She had vowed to leave for the States the day she turned sixteen.

"That is a long time," Niwot conceded. "But I can be patient. We will talk again, Grizzly Killer."

Nate watched the young warrior walk off. He was still angry, but his anger was tempered by the realization that when he was Niwot's age, he had been cocky and head-strong too. With a shrug he dismissed the incident. He had more important things to think about—namely, putting an end to Scar's gore-drenched spree.

A procession was winding among the lodges. Neota was at the head, a portrait in misery if ever there was one. One man beat a handheld drum in slow cadence while mourners keened and wailed.

Nate sat back down facing the river. Picking up a stone, he chucked it out into the current. He had known Star At Morning only a short while, but he had liked her, liked her a lot. To think that just yesterday she had been in the full bloom of life, bursting with beauty and vitality, and now she was a cold corpse that would soon rot and decay.

Here one minute, gone the next, Nate reflected. The ways of the world could be bitterly cruel. He counted his blessings that his wife, daughter, and son were hearty and hale. Losing any of them would crush him. He would much rather he were first to go than have to shed tears over their graves.

The village grew as quiet as a graveyard. Nate leaned back

on his hands and idly scanned the mountains to the south. Movement on a low ridge a quarter-mile off drew his attention. A large animal was meandering across it. An elk, he assumed, until it occurred to him the color of its coat was all wrong. As he looked on, it halted, and he saw it in full profile.

Nate couldn't believe his eyes. Only one animal was that size and that shape: a grizzly. And since no other griz would dare intrude on Scar's domain, it had to be the Ute-slayer himself. Heaving to his feet, Nate saw the bear paw at the ground as if digging. Maybe it was after pikas or other rodents. In which case it might be occupied for a while, giving him time to get there.

Pivoting, Nate dashed to the bay and yanked out the picket pin. He swung onto the saddle, lashed the reins, and plunged into the river. There was a ford a hundred yards downstream, but every second was crucial. The water rose only as high as the bay's brisket, and in less than a minute he was across and galloping hell-bent for leather toward the ridge.

Nate raced into a belt of cottonwoods and on through into thick pines. A thick carpet of needles muffled the drum of the bay's hooves. He lost sight of the ridge and prayed Scar would still be there when he could see it again. For once luck was with him. When the bay broke from the trees a hundred yards from the bottom of the ridge, Scar was still digging away.

Nate jerked the Hawken to his shoulder and just as quickly lowered it again. At that range and that angle, the odds of hitting a vital organ were slim.

On up the slope Nate sped. Scar suddenly stop digging. He thought the rogue glanced around at him, but he couldn't be sure. Scar bolted, barreling into the woods as if shot from a cannon.

Nate slapped his legs against the bay, spurring it on. Bears were faster than horses, but in the forest Scar couldn't attain his top speed. All Nate had to do was keep the griz in sight until it tired. Another factor in Nate's favor was that for all their speed over short distances, grizzlies lacked stamina. The bay had a good chance of outlasting the bastard.

In a flurry of driving hooves and flying clods of dirt, Nate reached the crest. Scar was sixty to seventy yards off and moving like a runaway carriage. Bending to avoid low limbs, Nate pushed the bay to its limit. Every few seconds he caught a glimpse of Scar's hindquarters. The bear had gained a little ground, but not enough to lose them.

The chase went on for the better part of a mile. Nate kept waiting for the bear to show signs of fatigue, but Scar held to a steady pace. Then the bay swept over a rise and below was a talus slope—and no Scar. Hauling on the reins, Nate brought the bay to a sliding stop. To the west grew weeds and barely enough trees to hide a goat. To the east were dense firs.

Nate rode east. Again and again he craned his neck for some sign of the monster. Again and again he was disappointed. Five minutes of headlong travel persuaded Nate he had blundered. The bear must have gone west.

"So close," Nate said softly to himself, slowing the bay. As if in answer, from out of the vegetation came a loud grunt. Reining up, he scoured the woods and spied a patch of brown fur several hundred feet off, traveling to the southeast. A few more seconds and he clearly saw the rogue's huge hump.

Scar was moving at a plodding walk, evidently unaware that Nate had caught up. Nate's first impulse was to gallop after the brute, but he held back. Here was a golden opportunity to get within rifle range. He mustn't squander it.

Waiting until Scar was almost out of sight, Nate slowly followed. The wind had died to a whisper, so he needn't worry Scar would pick up his scent. So long as Nate hung far enough back, Scar couldn't hear him either.

Long minutes dragged by. Nate needed the bear to stop so he could sneak close enough for a shot. But Scar trudged tirelessly on, his shoulder muscles rippling with every ponderous step.

So long as they were moving through thick forest Nate

was reasonably safe from detection. But presently the woodland thinned and Scar headed up a grassy slope toward a broad shelf. Nate didn't dare show himself. Champing at the bit like a thoroughbred, he bided his time.

Just as Scar was on the verge of going over the shelf, he halted and sniffed. Afraid the bear would bolt again, Nate inwardly swore. But he need not have worried. Scar had caught the scent of something, sure enough, but it wasn't him. Angling to the southwest, the bear was soon out of sight.

Nate counted to thirty before riding on. He was taking a risk, but as the old saying had it, better safe than sorry. At a point a few yards below the shelf, he halted and rose in the stirrups. Beyond was an aspen grove, the leaves shimmering brightly in the sunlight. From its depths issued a series of grunts.

More wary than ever, Nate rode into the grove. The aspens grew so close together, they limited his range of vision. Scar might be fifty yards ahead or might be fifteen. And to make matters more perilous, the wind had increased and was shifting.

Nate drew rein every ten yards or so to look and listen. The grunting had stopped, which might mean the griz was out of earshot—or about to jump him. The bay had its ears pricked, but it wasn't acting unduly agitated.

Suddenly a jay squawked to the southwest. The undergrowth crackled as a distinctive silhouette broke from cover and lit out like its backside was on fire.

Scar knew Nate was there. It was no use trying to sneak up on him. A jab of Nate's heels spurred the bay to a gallop. He rode with reckless disregard for their safety, determined Scar wouldn't get away. The bear was running full out again and soon had gained on them, but not enough to lose them.

"Not this time, damn you," Nate declared.

Clusters of dense brush randomly barred Scar's path, but he went through them as if they weren't there.

Nate could see the grizzly a little more clearly, enough to tell the rogue wasn't quite as huge as he thought. He kept

Join the Western Book Club and GET 4 FREE* BOOKS NOW!
A $19.96 VALUE!

Yes! I want to subscribe to the Western Book Club.

Please send me my **4 FREE* BOOKS**. I have enclosed $2.00 for shipping/handling. Each month I'll receive the four newest Leisure Western selections to preview for 10 days. If I decide to keep them, I will pay the Special Members Only discounted price of just $3.36 each, a total of $13.44, plus $2.00 shipping/handling ($19.50 US in Canada). This is a **SAVINGS OF AT LEAST $6.00** off the bookstore price. There is no minimum number of books I must buy, and I may cancel the program at any time. In any case, the **4 FREE* BOOKS** are mine to keep.

*In Canada, add $5.00 shipping/handling per order for the first shipment. For all future shipments to Canada, the cost of membership is $16.25 US, which includes shipping and handling. (All payments must be made in US dollars.)

NAME: _____

ADDRESS: _____

CITY: _____ STATE: _____

COUNTRY: _____ ZIP: _____

TELEPHONE: _____

E-MAIL: _____

SIGNATURE: _____

hoping Scar would glance back so he could get a good look at the hideous visage the Utes had gone on about, but Scar wouldn't oblige.

A steep slope marked the end of the aspens. Scar took it on the fly. He was heading up the mountain, as he had the day before. Nate wondered if he was making for the same ravine. But no. For soon Scar changed direction to the southeast, with heightened urgency, as if he had a specific destination in mind and was anxious to reach it before he tired.

About thirty yards was all that separated them. Several times Nate had a clear shot at the bear's backside and hump, but both were too thick with muscle to waste lead on. A broadside or head-on shot was best.

Scar came to a boulder-strewn tableland and vanished around one twice as big as he was. Beyond were dozens more, a veritable maze in which the grizzly could lose himself.

Nate brought the bay to a stop. No sane person would go in there but he had come too far to give up. Throwing his left leg over the saddle, he slid down. Caution demanded he proceed on foot. On horseback he would make too much noise. Gliding to the nearest boulder, he pressed his back to it. The only sound was the wind, but Nate was willing to bet every dollar he ever earned that the bear was in there somewhere, waiting for him. Thumbing back the hammer, he stalked into the boulder field.

Nate rounded a second boulder, then a third. He was almost to the fourth when he thought to examine the ground and was rewarded with as fine a set of prints as he could ask for, perfectly outlined in the dust. Renewed hope surged in his breast. Scar had finally made a mistake. The tracks would lead him right to where the griz was hiding.

Scarcely breathing, Nate wound deeper and deeper into the labyrinth. The distance between the prints showed him Scar had still been moving fast, but a little farther on the silvertip had stopped and shifted to see if Nate was still after him. From there the tracks bore to the right, between a large

David Thompson

pair of boulders. Nate started to follow, then paused. A feeling came over him, a certainty that Scar was just beyond, poised to pounce. Slanting to the left, he went around instead. He had only a few yards to go when a great head reared skyward and a roar broke the stillness.

Instantly Nate fired. Expecting Scar to charge, he skipped backward, dropped his rifle, and palmed both flintlocks.

A gurgling growl, the rattle of rocks, and quiet fell again.

Nate crouched with his pistols extended, braced for the bear's rush. But it never came. As it began to dawn on him that the bear must have fled, he crept past the twin boulders to check for sign of blood. What he found was the answer to his prayers.

The boulders were perched on the rim of a cliff. Two hundred feet below, dashed among jagged rocks, lay the terror of Ute territory.

Chapter Nine

Nate King seldom felt proud of killing an animal. Usually he did so to put food on his family's table. Sometimes he had to slay to preserve his life or the lives of others. They were routine occurrences, an integral part of life in the wilderness, and once done, largely forgotten. But today Nate felt immense pride. He had done it. He had slain the beast responsible for bringing so much sorrow and suffering to the Utes. Untold lives had been saved. So he could be excused for feeling immense personal satisfaction for a job well done. He held his head high as he came to the river bordering the Ute encampment, and smiled as he forded it.

The Utes were back. The ceremony had concluded and they were listlessly standing about, awaiting the command to take down their lodges and prepare for the long ride to a new site. Someone spotted Nate and a shout went up. By the time he came to the far bank, Hototo and a dozen others were waiting for him.

"Why are you so happy?" the old hawk-eyed warrior signed.

David Thompson

"Where is Neota?" Nate responded.

"Over by what is left of his lodge."

The Ute leader was on his knees amid the debris, sifting through it for personal effects that had not been damaged. He found a small doll and held it close to his breast, his eyes closed. But he opened them as the bay came to a stop, and reverently set it down so he could sign, "I have made a decision, Grizzly Killer. It was wrong of me to impose on you. Scar is our problem. We must deal with him ourselves. You can leave whenever you like and there will be no hard feelings."

"I will go soon enough, but only because my work here is done. Scar has killed his last human being."

Neota's eyes narrowed, then widened in budding amazement. "You cannot mean what I think you mean."

"Would you like to see his body?"

Hototo and others had witnessed the exchange, and an excited flurry of voices broke out. Yells were raised. Word spread through the village like a prairie wildfire, and Utes rushed from all over to hear for themselves. Their sadness gave way to smiles of heartfelt joy. Some burst into tears of happiness. Many embraced one another.

Neota slowly rose and came over to the bay. "My head tells my heart this cannot be, yet my heart knows you always speak with a straight tongue. Yes, I would very much like to see the killer of my family up close. I will help you skin him and dry the meat for your trip home."

"The meat I give to your people," Nate signed. "The hide is yours to do with as you will."

"I have nothing to give you in return."

"The gift of your friendship is enough."

Neota looked away and coughed, then clutched Nate's hand. There and then an unbreakable bond was forged between them. Nate had a new friend for as long as they both should live.

Hototo had been talking to others. "Everyone would like to see Scar's body. I suggest we make a travois and haul it back. How far is it to where you slew him, Grizzly Killer?"

"We can be there and back by dark," Nate answered. But retrieving the mangled remains would pose a problem. He had not seen any way down to the bottom of the cliff.

Composing himself, Neota turned to Hototo. "Select twenty men to accompany us. Tonight our people feast. Tonight we celebrate as we have never celebrated before."

"But the period of mourning for your wife and daughters—" the old warrior signed.

"Were they able to speak for themselves, they would agree with me. For too long have our people lived in fear. Tonight we must banish it from our hearts." Neota strode toward the horse herd.

Hototo frowned and signed to Nate, "I do not like it. Grief must be shared or it festers like a boil. He must not keep his in."

Nate had long been intigued by the differing attitudes of the white and red cultures. Their outlooks on land, on marriage, on the rearing of children, and on life itself, were worlds apart. He had been raised to believe a man bottled up his grief and kept it pent-in his whole life long. Crying was considered unseemly. In contrast, quite a few Indian tribes indulged in public outpourings of sadness on certain occasions, and it was not uncommon at such times to see tears stain the cheeks of grown warriors.

The village bustled with activity. The warriors chosen by Hototo hurried to their lodges for their weapons, while their sons rushed to fetch their horses. Women were gathering in groups to revel in the good news.

Nate rode to the river to wait. He figured the Utes would want him to stay the night and take part in their celebration. But come morning he was heading for home. Leaning on the pommel, he smiled. All the tension had drained from him like water from a sieve. He felt truly at ease for the first time in weeks.

The warriors lost no time in getting ready. Nate nodded at Neota and Hototo, then guided the bay across the river. Niwot was also along, but Nate ignored him. The sooner the youth realized his interest in Evelyn wasn't appreciated, the better for all of them.

Years of life in the wild had given Nate the instincts of a homing pigeon. Once he had been somewhere, he never forgot how to get there. Unerringly, he led the Utes to the boulder field, and from the cliff rim they gazed down in sober silence on the legend laid low.

"It is over at last," Neota signed.

"His neck must be broken," Hototo observed. "See how the head is bent under the body?"

The cliff ran for hundreds of feet in both directions, ending in treacherous talus slopes. Neota dispatched warriors to find a way to the bottom, then squatted and stared at the shattered body of the creature that had cost him so dearly. "The tale of your deed, Grizzly Killer, will be told around our lodge fires for as long as my people live.

Nate hunkered beside him. Luck, more than anything else, had accounted for Scar's comeuppance. Being in the right place at the right time, and spotting the griz on the ridge. "I am happy to do what I could. Now your people can sleep in peace at night."

Neota's features darkened. "Not all of them."

Nate thought of Star At Morning, so radiant, so lovely, and those three adorable girls. Four innocents, snuffed out like candles. The injustice of it all brought a sour taste to his mouth. It tried a man's soul to think that the Almighty permitted such atrocities.

Evelyn once asked Nate why bad things happened to good people. He told her that some folks believed it was God's way of testing people. Others, that God was punishing them. Still others felt that after setting creation in order, the Almighty no longer took a direct hand and bad things just happened. Then there was a fourth view that held God didn't exist and never had, and that the bad was the natural order of things.

"What do you think, Pa?" Evelyn had persisted.

"I honestly don't know, daughter," Nate admitted, and had been stung by the disappointment in her eyes. But he'd always striven to be honest with her, and he wasn't about to deceive her by claiming knowledge he didn't possess. "I've pondered on it a lot. Most any thinking person has. And I'm no closer now to understanding why things are the way they are than I was when I was your age."

"But you've lived so long, seen so much," Evelyn noted. "You've read the Bible through and through."

"It raised as many questions as it answered," Nate had said, placing a hand on her shoulder. "I'm sorry. When you were younger, you always thought your ma and I had answers to everything. But the truth is, we don't."

The clatter of hooves ended Nate's reverie. Warriors were returning. They had found a trail to the bottom. Everyone mounted up, and within half an hour they were at the bottom of the cliff and drawing rein two dozen yards from the dead grizzly. They couldn't get any closer on horseback, because their animals had caught Scar's scent and were shying and balking.

Nate wanted to be the first there. Scaling a boulder, he hopped from one to another until he was next to the body. The smell of blood was thick in the air. From Scar's hump and back protruded the jagged ends of broken bones. The neck was bent under the shoulders, hiding the hideous face. Nate gripped the bear's blood-soaked fur and tugged, but he couldn't straighten it.

The Utes surrounded their former nemesis. No one said a word until Neota moved in close, signing, "Allow us, Grizzly Killer."

It took five husky warriors to lift the body high enough for Neota and several others to pull the head from underneath. Almost to a man, they recoiled in consternation. Neota dropped to his knees and flung his arms to the sky as if to scream, "Why? Why? Why?"

Nate gaped in astonishment, his mind awhirl with the implications.

"Do not feel bad, Grizzly Killer," Hototo signed. "Anyone could have made the same mistake."

It wasn't Scar. The skull had partially caved in and both

eyes had popped from their sockets, but the head was intact enough for Nate to tell it was otherwise perfectly normal. There was no hairless skin, not a single scar.

"Who would have thought another bear was in our valley?" Hototo tried to soothe him. "Scar was the first we had seen in a long time."

Suddenly Nate remembered the nocturnal prowler that paid his camp a visit the night before he arrived. He was sure it had been a bear. That was the same night Sakima's family was slain and Sakima's wife dragged off. Since not even Scar could be in two places at once, he should have guessed there was another bear in the area.

Neota had slumped forward, his forehead resting on the boulder, but suddenly he pushed to his feet and signed, "I agree, Grizzly Killer. You cannot blame yourself." An icy smile spread across his face. "In a way I am glad. Now I have the chance to kill Scar myself."

Nate felt like a prized dunce. He had been remiss in not making sure before he rode to the village and broke the news. The women and children would be devastated to learn the monster was still on the loose. "I apologize to your people for my stupidity. And I give them my word I will not rest until I bring them Scar's head on a pole."

"We will start tomorrow," Neota signed. "I will bring extra horses. Once we flush Scar, we will ride them in relays and chase him until he is too exhausted to go another step. Then I can have my revenge."

It was an old trick. The Comanches used it to catch wild horses. The Shoshones used it on occasion to run down buffalo. But Nate was skeptical it would work on a grizzly. For one thing, mustangs and buffalo favored the open plains, not dense woodland. For another, grizzlies were much more apt to turn on their pursuers. But until he could come up with a better idea, he shouldn't nitpick. "I will be ready to ride out when you are."

The wind, always Scar's friend, alerted him to the presence of his enemies. He was asleep in a thicket high on a north-facing slope when his nose registered the scent of Feather Heads. Instantly he raised his head and sniffed. The wind was from the northwest, the scent faint, which told him the direction and gave him some inkling of the distance. They posed no danger.

Scar was about to lower his head and resume his nap when another, fainter, scent brought him upright with every nerve vibrant. As soon as he rose, he lost it. He moved a few steps to the left and sniffed, but he couldn't pick it up. He lumbered to the right with the same result.

Frustrated, Scar headed lower. Feather Heads or no, he had to find out. Only a few Warblers and Bushy Tails were abroad. Scar never liked the abuse the Bushy Tails heaped on him, but they always stayed high in the trees, well out of his reach, so he ignored them. The scent of the Feather Heads grew stronger. But try as he might, Scar couldn't detect the scent that had mattered more.

The wind died, and Scar halted. He had come far enough. Without the wind he could never pick up the scent again, if it had been there at all. His infallible nose might finally have been wrong. Then a gust ruffled the fur on his neck and brought with it the undeniable odor he knew so well. Head craned, Scar moved from side to side. He established that the scent came from the same direction as that of the Feather Heads, and concern launched him down the mountain at a trot.

Memories stirred. Memories of the den time, the happiest of his life. Of playing with his brother and sister. Of Caregiver leading the three of them off on new grand adventures into the outside world. He thought of those times often. He dreamed of them often. And now he was being reminded of them again by a scent out of his past.

The babble of Feather Heads slowed Scar to a wary walk. They were below the next slope, among boulders at the base of a cliff. He could not quite tell what they were doing, but it involved their short shiny sticks. Their scent, combined with that of fresh blood, had smothered the other scent. He circled to the west to go around and resume his search, but stopped when the Feather Heads began filing to their Manes. Soon they rode off. Among them, Scar noticed at the last moment, was Wood Eater Head.

Scar let them go. He was interested only in that special scent. Continuing westward, he happened to look toward the base of the cliff. A carcass lay there, the remains of an animal stripped of its hide and much of its meat. White bone glistened in the sun, from which stringy flesh clung loosely.

Scar took the slope at a lope. Near the bottom the familiar scent returned, but so faint he could barely smell it. The odor of the Feather Heads, the droppings of their Manes, and puddles of blood were partly to blame. The other reason emptied Scar's mind of conscious thought and numbed him as Caregiver's death so long ago had done. Slowly, almost timidly, he climbed onto the boulders and over to what was left of the body. There the familiar scent was strongest. He stared at the grisly husk that had once been one of his own kind. At the husk that had once been his brother.

Were it not for the faint scent that clung to the remains, Mean would be unrecognizable. His eyes had been cut off when the hide was removed and lay drawing flies in the dirt. His chest had been carved clean of meat clear down to the ribs, as had his haunches. All four limbs were attached, but his forelegs were broken in several places and the Feather Heads had snipped the claws from all his paws.

Scar backed away. Leaving the boulders, he entered a stand of pines and sank onto his stomach. He had always wanted to run into Mean again but never had. Once, many seasons past, he saw Nice, but she had wanted nothing to do with him. He had been catching his fill in a fish-choked river when a cub appeared. Since he never developed a taste for his own kind, he ignored it. But it started bawling anyway, and out of the briars came its incensed mother. She roared and waded in after him. Scar had no inclination to give up his fishing spot and was set to hold his ground—until he caught her scent. The surprise, along with her flying paws, caused him to retreat to the bank, where he stood and waited for her to recognize him. But if she had caught his scent, she gave no sign of it. Rising on her rear legs, she roared all the louder, giving every indication she would rip into him if he dared come any closer.

His own sister.

Scar had no desire to hurt Nice, so he left. He came back the next day and every day thereafter until the leaves changed color, hoping she would return, but she never did. That was the last contact he had with any of his family—until now.

The cold fury that always lurked deep inside Scar spread outward from his core. There was no end to the Feather Heads' savagery. Nor would there be an end to his. Starting that very night, he would stalk and slay until his coat ran scarlet with their blood. He would never stop so long as a Feather Head remained alive.

Rising, Scar headed for the trail his brother's slayers had taken. They had a head start, but that was all right. He knew where they were bound. By nightfall he would reach the river, and soon after the killing would begin.

An aura of impending doom hung over the Ute encampment. The news that Scar was still alive hit them like an avalanche, smothering their newfound joy and crushing their spirit. Most went into their lodges and stayed there. The few who moved about did so listlessly, all their vitality sapped. Their despair was as boundless as their happiness had been only a few hours ago.

Nate was treated as if he had contracted the plague. His hosts deliberately avoided him as he strolled about the village. They would turn their backs, or veer aside so as not to pass anywhere near him. Not one would meet his gaze.

Nate didn't hold it against them. He never should have announced that Scar was dead without verifying it. Neota had tried to boost their morale with a short speech, but it was greeted with stony silence. Soon after, he disappeared, and now Nate was trying to find him so they could head out again after Scar.

A complete circuit of the village failed to turn up Neota,

and Nate ended up back at his horses. He was anxious to be shed of the place, and annoyed he had to stick around waiting for Neota to show. Squatting, he poked at the ground with a twig until footsteps approached from the rear. "About time," he said to himself, and rose. But it wasn't whom he expected.

Hototo was holding a flat piece of wood on which rested several strips of roast venison and a generous portion of dried berries. He held it out, and when Nate accepted, he signed, "My woman thought you might be hungry, Grizzly Killer."

Nate didn't have much of an appetite, but he sat down with the plate across his legs and responded, "Thank her for me." It was touching that someone should be so thoughtful after what he had done. Selecting a warm strip, he bit into the juicy meat. Spices had been added for extra flavor.

Hototo hunkered in front of him. "Please do not be angry at my people. If you had been through what they have, you would understand why they treat you as they do."

"I hold no grudge." Nate understood all too well. He was mad at himself, not at the Utes. "Please let them know I am sorry."

"They already do," Hototo responded. "They do not avoid you because they hate you. Have you not noticed they also avoid one another? Their hearts are broken. They stay in their lodges like turtles in their shells, staring at the walls with empty eyes. I have never seen such a thing in all the winters of my life. Should Scar attack again tonight, I fear they will not lift a finger to defend themselves."

Nate thoughtfully bit off another piece. The old warrior had a point. Scar had struck two nights running. It made sense the rogue would pay the village another visit tonight.

"There are times when I think Scar is not a bear at all. That he is not flesh and blood but a shade from the other side sent to torment us."

"You have seen its tracks with your own eyes. Spirits do not leave footprints."

"Who among us can say with certainty what spirits can and cannot do? In a lake to the west lives a spirit creature that cannot be killed. It capsizes canoes and eats those in them. And when it comes on shore it leaves tracks, just like Scar does. But everyone knows it is not flesh and blood as we are."

The Shoshones, too, believed in the existence of several lake creatures to which they ascribed supernatural abilities. Nate had never seen one, himself, although he would dearly love to. "Scar can be killed," he insisted. He gazed out across the sea of lodges, wondering which Scar would pick next and how he could prevent it. The next second insight washed over him with the icy sensation of a frigid mountain stream. "We have been going about this all wrong. So did the other bands."

Hototo looked at him expectantly.

"Scar has always been able to do as he pleases. He attacks and then disappears in the forest, forcing your people to go after him. Forcing them to fight him in his element. Why not make him fight in yours?"

"I have lost your sign."

"The village is your element. It is where your people are strongest. Tonight when Scar attacks we must use that against him. We must set a trap to prevent him from getting out of the village alive."

Hototo was clearly interested in the proposal. "How do you suggest we do this? By making large fires so we can see him coming?"

"No. That would only scare him off. We want him to think the village is the same as it was last night and the night before." Setting down the bark plate, Nate stood and pivoted a full three hundred and sixty degrees, contemplating the possibilities. It would take considerable work, but it could be done. "Find Neota. Have him call a council and submit my idea to them. For it to work, everyone in the village must work together."

"It will be done."

The old warrior was as good as his word. Every warrior

in the band wanted to be in on the meeting, but there wasn't room for all of them in the lodge, so a huge crowd gathered around it, with updates relayed by those near the entrance. An air of excitement gripped the village. The emotional lethargy that had them in its thrall had been broken.

The council lasted a quarter of an hour. Neota led a delegation of leaders and elders to where Nate was waiting, and expressed the outcome succinctly by signing, "What would you have us do?"

Nate had been giving it a lot of thought. He had Neota divide the warriors into groups. One group went into the forest to chop down trees and strip the limbs. Another was set to work digging pits, one near the riverbank to the south and another near the river to the east. Those were the directions in which Scar had left the village previously, and if the grizzly managed to break out of their trap, Nate was hopeful it would choose one or the other again.

Women were set to work collecting firewood, which Nate had them pile at several locations within the village. Others sharpened the stakes that would be embedded in the bottom of the pits. The older children were told to cut suitable lengths of rope to be used in the construction of half a dozen fifteen-foot platforms, one at each point of the compass along the outer perimeter and two more toward the middle of the village. Younger children were instructed to gather every buffalo robe and bear hide to be found in every lodge.

As Nate walked among them, checking on their progress, he was treated to friendly smiles of appreciation. He returned them, and encouraged the workers with sign talk, spreading the message that if all went well, tonight would be the last night of Scar's existence.

Even with every living soul in the village involved, it was after sunset before the work was done. Neota called his people together to impart Nate's detailed instructions, and then the Utes went to their assigned positions.

Everything was set.

Now all they could do was wait.

*   *   *

Scar was in no great hurry to reach the Feather Head lair. Since he couldn't cross the river undetected until dark, he took his time getting there. Stars speckled the sky when he came to the last hill and halted to test the wind. All appeared normal. Smoke wafted from many of the cones, and a few Feather Heads were moving about.

As silently as a whisper of wind, Scar descended to the near riverbank. Memories of how his mother and brother had died gnawed at him, and he gnashed his great teeth together in anticipation of the flesh he would soon rip and rend. Placing a giant paw into the water, he stopped.

Scar's infallible nose tingled with the scent of Shaggies and Lesser Bears. Such scents were typical of the Feather Heads, but tonight the odors were stronger than they had ever been. He twisted his head, sniffing and analyzing, and when he detected nothing else out of the ordinary, he started across the river.

Halfway across, Scar halted again. There was a tree on the opposite bank where there had never been a tree before. Peering closer, he saw that it wasn't a tree at all but something the Feather Heads had built, much as they did their cones. Rising onto his hind legs to better catch the breeze, he sniffed and sniffed, but all he smelled was the same scent he did when Wood Eaters gnawed down trees. Whatever it was, it did not pose a threat.

Dropping onto all fours, Scar quietly waded to the opposite shore and was almost to the top of the embankment when a jumble of new odors reached him. He smelled more gnawed wood, and cropped grass, and the scent of many Feather Heads, shes and young alike. They had been near that spot not long ago, but they were gone now.

Scar raised his head high enough to see over the bank. The odors were strongest to his left, where a large patch of ground looked different from the rest. Grass and leaves had been scattered for a purpose that eluded him. It looked harmless enough, but he did not like it. Warily, he levered his huge body up over the rim and bore to the right to avoid it.

David Thompson

The warble of a bird from atop the tree the Feather Heads had made brought Scar up short. He listened intently, but it was not repeated, and his nose gave him no reason to be alarmed. Moving on, he passed between two cones. He saw more strange trees and something else, something that raised the hackles along his neck. Near many of the cones, low to the ground, were peculiar hairy humps. Never, in all the times he had visited Feather Head lairs, had he seen anything like them. They appeared to be the hides of Shaggies and Lesser Bears, and accounted for the uncommonly strong odors of both. But like the strange trees, the reason they were there was a mystery.

So were the tall piles of branches Scar now discovered. One was close by, and he glimpsed others farther off.

An impulse to turn and leave welled within him. Too much was new, too much uncertain. But countering the impulse was his urge to slay more Feather Heads. To feel his claws shear through their fragile bodies and his mouth fill with their blood. He moved on, stopping frequently to sniff and cock his head for sounds. Instead of penetrating to the center of the lair, as he had intended, Scar stalked toward the next cone.

The Feather Heads inside were about to die.

Chapter Ten

Nate King was flat on his stomach on one of the platforms erected in the middle of the village when a warrior on a platform near the river warbled like a robin. He raised his head and glanced at Neota. They had been lying there for about an hour and a half, waiting for a signal from the perimeter lookouts.

The trap had been sprung.

Neota nudged Nate and nodded toward an inky mass on the east riverbank. The chief reached for one of the special arrows that lay between them. Arrows whose barbed tips had been wrapped tight with strips of buckskin sprinkled with black powder from Nate's powder horn. On each platform were several similar arrows, not to be used until Neota gave the signal.

The inky mass left the bank. Gradually the silhouette of the giant bear took form and substance. Nate could not see it all that well, and he hoped to God it was actually Scar and not some other bear that had happened by. He slid a finger through the Hawken's trigger guard and wedged the heavy stock to his shoulder.

David Thompson

The man-killer had stopped between two of the outermost lodges. Near both were the huddled figures of warriors and armed women hidden under buffalo robes and bear hides to mask their scent.

Neota hadn't liked the idea of the women helping out. He had balked until an older woman pointed out that it was customary for the women of their tribe to help defend their villages from enemy attack. Whether that enemy was a hostile war party or a grizzly should be irrelevant.

Hototo translated her eloquent appeal for Nate's benefit. Neota reluctantly gave in, and made a short speech in which he asked for female volunteers but stressed no one would hold it against them if they refused. Every last woman stepped forward.

Now Neota was nocking the special arrow to his ash bow. But he did not raise the bow to shoot it. He put both down, picked up two pieces of quartz, and held them poised over the treated buckskin, ready to rub them together at the proper moment. On the other platforms other warriors would be doing the same.

Timing was everything. Nate watched Scar closely, waiting for the grizzly to move deeper into the village. Instead, moments later, the silvertip crept toward a lodge only a few dozen yards from the river. Nate immediately tapped Neota's shoulder. The chief only had to strike the pieces of quartz together three times before a spark ignited the black powder, and the entire strip of buckskin combusted in a flash of red and orange.

Neota swiftly raised the bow and drew the sinew string back past his ear. He took aim, but not at Scar. He sighted down his arrow at the pile of firewood nearest the bear, and his bow string twanged.

The fire arrow streaked through the night, crackling and hissing like a molten meteorite plunging to earth from the ethereal void of space. It struck the firewood dead center and lodged fast. The deadwood caught immediately. Within seconds other fire arrows flashed from other platforms to strike other piles of firewood. Flames leaped high, dispelling the darkness and revealing the ursine intruder in all his horrific majesty.

Scar had not moved. He stood staring at the nearest bonfire as if mesmerized, and for the first time Nate saw the demon clearly: the mighty sinews that corded the grizzly's gigantic frame, the powerful paws that could crush a human skull without half trying, the wicked, knife-sized claws that could shred a man like so much straw. Nate also saw the scarred, hairless, hideous countenance that gave small children nightmares and grown men goose bumps.

Neota had notched a normal arrow to his bow. Leaping erect, he moved to the edge of the platform, cupped his right hand to his mouth, and uttered a piercing war whoop. On cue, the warriors and women hidden under the buffalo robes and bear hides cast them off and leaped up, brandishing their weapons.

For a few moments the tableau was carved from granite.

Then Scar roared a roar such as had not been heard since the beginning of time, a roar that seemed to shake the platform on which Nate was rising and buffeted the air about him. Over three-fourths of a ton of solid muscle hurled itself at the nearest Utes, and before any could scarce lift a finger to defend themselves, they had been reduced to mangled gore. Others rushed in, heedless of their safety, unleashing arrows and hurling lances. At the same time, the warriors on the closest platforms let fly with a stream of glittering barbed shafts.

A veritable hailstorm of deadly missiles transfixed Scar from every direction. His next roar, incredibly enough, was louder than before, as with blinding fury he tore into the Utes anew. A warrior went down, his torso ripped open from throat to navel. A woman screamed as her head was separated from her shoulders. Another warrior lost an arm, and a second woman was skewered like a slice of meat.

As yet Nate hadn't fired. His was the most powerful weapon the Utes had at their disposal, and he did not want to waste the lead. But now, as he went to take precise aim, he discovered he didn't have a clear shot. Too many Utes were swarming around Scar in a constant swirl of thrusting lances, swinging war clubs, and glittering knives. It was all part of his plan to try and drive the bear toward one of the pits.

Neota glanced at him and spoke urgently in the Ute tongue.

Nate knew he was being urged to fire before more Utes lost their lives, but the only parts of the grizzly he could see clearly were its hump and the upper portion of its skull. Both were poor targets. The hump was a solid mass of muscle, the skull thick enough to deflect most bullets.

Again Neota urged him to fire.

Another warrior went down, his stomach ripped out.

"Damn!" Nate declared. Taking a bead on the crown of the rogue's head, he fired. Blood spurted, but he couldn't tell if the ball had penetrated or not.

Suddenly Scar rose up on his hind legs and gave voice to another tremendous roar. The new wound had incited him beyond measure. He swatted Utes down as fast as they appeared in front of him, crushing, slashing, flaying.

Undaunted, the Utes continued to rain arrows, lances, and clubs on their nemesis. They were as incensed as Scar, if not more so. The suffering he had caused, the deaths and havoc, had taken a severe emotional toll. And now all their feelings were being released in a paroxysm of unbridled violence. Every warrior, every woman, fought with a savagery terrible to behold.

Neota shouted something and dashed to the pole they had used to climb to the top of the platform. Slinging his bow across a shoulder, he gripped the pole with both hands, swung his legs over the side, and slid rapidly to the ground.

Nate was busy reloading. His rifle was still their best bet of bringing the bear down. His fingers flew as he poured black powder down the barrel, then inserted a ball and patch into the muzzle. Jerking the ramrod from its housing under the barrel, he quickly tamped the ball all the way down.

In the meantime, the battle had reached a crescendo. Utes

were pouring from all parts of the village in a valiant attempt to end the bear's reign of horror once and for all. A score or more were down, dead or dying, but that did not stop the rest.

As for Scar, arrows and lances bristled from his huge frame like quills from a porcupine. He was bleeding from countless wounds, and his hide was more red than brown. Yet his rage would not be denied. He plowed through the Utes like a harrow through soft earth, his blood-flecked teeth and flesh-spattered claws exacting a fearsome toll.

Nate shoved the ramrod into its housing. Moving to the edge, he rose on the tips of his toes and again tried to take aim at Scar's vitals, only to be thwarted by the press of Utes. Anxious to try and help, he turned toward the pole.

Scar abruptly sent a dozen of them tumbling, opening a gap in their ranks. For a few fleeting seconds his left side was fully exposed. In the blink of an eye Nate sighted and fired. He went for a lung shot since the angle was best, and this time he scored. The grizzly stumbled, and his great head dipped. Stumbled, but he did not go down.

Regaining his balance, Scar spun toward the river and charged headlong into the Ute ranks. They parted, and for a moment Nate thought they were breaking and running. But no, they were doing as he had instructed, and opening an avenue that would funnel the bear toward one of the deep pits. And, if all went well, impale him on the sharp stakes at the bottom.

Nate ran to the pole and slid down so fast, he blistered his right palm. There was no time to reload the Hawken. Drawing one of his pistols, he raced to join the melee and do his part to drive the rogue into the pit.

That Scar still lived was a testament to his enormous vitality and indomitable will. He had sustained wounds grave enough to kill a dozen of his kind, yet he did not fall, did not slacken. He was elemental ferocity incarnate.

Nate reached the whirlwind fringe of the conflict. So many Utes were in front of him, he couldn't get anywhere near the bear to use his pistol. They were stabbing and clubbing and shouting in a mad bedlam, but bedlam with an ulterior design. For bit by bit they were forcing the bear toward the grass and leaves that covered his impending doom. Another ten to fifteen yards and they would drive Scar over the lip. His own weight would crash him through the latticework of thin branches and it would be over.

But Scar was not a sheep to be meekly led to slaughter. The Utes paid, and paid dearly, for every yard. Women as well as men threw themselves at him in potential sacrifice of their lives for the potential greater good of ending his. Foremost among them was Neota, wielding a war club with devastating effect. His face had been transformed. Gone was the calm, gentle warrior who had so impressed Nate with his noble bearing. The calmness had been replaced by an unquenchable thirst for vengeance, the gentleness by a wanton need to kill, kill, kill.

Only five yards now between Scar and the pit. But they were five yards too many. The bear had set himself and would not be moved. His forepaws beat a bloody tempo on those who came too near. Those his claws did not maim or slay, his teeth did.

Nate jumped high into the air to see above the tangle. He had a decent shot if only the Utes would move aside and give it to him. But that was not to be, not in the state they were in. So he did the next best thing. He jumped into the air a second time, and yet a third, and at the apex he snap-aimed and fired.

Another roar greeted the blast. Scar half reared, then spun. For several heart-lifting moments it appeared he would blunder straight into the pit. But at the last split second, as if warned by some sixth sense, Scar veered to the right and gave it a wide berth. Arrows and lances sought his back and sides, but he reached the riverbank and plunged on over in a spray of dirt.

Howling and whooping, the Utes rushed after him. They stopped at the water's edge, for by then Scar had almost gained the other side. When he did, he did not look back.

Limping badly, he lumbered into the benighted woods and was swallowed by the vegetation.

Nate bowed his head and closed his eyes, overcome by disappointment. His plan had failed. The bear still lived, and while stricken, might eventually recover and resume preying on the Utes. He had let them down, and he could not bring himself to look any of them in the face. Then, through his fog of regret, rose lusty cheers and cries of happiness, and he glanced up to find the Utes laughing and clapping one another on the back and generally acting as if it were the most wonderful day of their lives.

Neota came toward him, grinning broadly, and enthusiastically thumped him on the shoulders. "We thank you, Grizzly Killer!" he signed.

"For what?" Nate responded after shoving the pistol under his belt and leaning his rifle against his leg.

"Did you not see? No bear can live after that! Scar will crawl off to die. At last we need no longer live in fear."

Nate wished he felt as confident. He was about to ask if they weren't being premature, but Neota had gone on by and was congratulating others. Deeply troubled, he stared into the dark depths of the wilderness as the deliriously giddy Utes began to drift back into their village. At dawn he would head out again. Wounded as Scar was, tracking should be easy. The blood trail alone should lead him right to where the grizzly was holed up.

A hand fell on Nate's left shoulder, and he turned.

It was Niwot, of all people, and he was frowning. "You are not smiling like the rest, Grizzly Killer. Can it be you share my belief this is not yet over?"

"I learned many winters ago never to count an animal as dead until I have seen its body," Nate signed.

"You are going after him, then?"

"At first light."

"I will go with you, if you do not mind."

Nate would rather have anyone else tag along than the upstart. But he thought it commendable of the young warrior to offer. "Thank you. But I prefer to hunt him alone, if you do not mind."

Niwot smirked and pointed at a gravel bar awash in starlight. "I will meet you there when the birds begin to sing." He walked off, nipping any debate in the bud.

Nate resented being treated so cavalierly by someone not even half his age. But if the young fool wanted to come, let him.

The mirth and shouts of joy were dying out. In their initial euphoria the Utes had overlooked the cost of their victory. But now, as they moved among the fallen, the terrible price was graven on their souls. Flickering light from the bonfires lit the ghastly scene as brilliantly as the noonday sun, showing every ruptured torso, severed limb, and pool of blood in vivid relief. Dozens had been victim to the bear's slashing claws and rending fangs. Many had breathed their last; others had been grievously wounded; a fortunate few sustained only broken bones or minor cuts.

Nate walked over to help and was riveted in stunned sorrow by the first body he came to. Hototo was on his back, his abdomen split open like a ripe melon. In his stiffening right hand he still clutched the broken stub of a lance. His lips were drawn back from his teeth, and his once-wise eyes were as vacant as a blank slate.

"No," Nate said softly, and squatted to close the old man's eyelids.

A profound quiet claimed the village. The Utes tended to their fellows, who bore their wounds in stoic silence. One woman, whose arm had been bitten clean off, had her teeth clenched so tightly that blood trickled from her gums. Yet she did not cry out. A warrior who had lost the lower half of a leg lay there without complaint.

From the lodges came the older women and children. Some could not hold back their tears, and once a few started weeping, a contagion of crying spread, so that soon sorrow was again widespread.

Nate moved out of the light and over to a dark spot near the river. He blamed himself for the loss of so many gallant, fine people. He knew there would be deaths, but he had not anticipated losing so many. He thought a withering deluge of lances and arrows would quickly drive the grizzly into one of the pits. In his arrogance he had forgotten the cardinal rule of dealing with bears. As his mentor, Shakespeare McNair, once phrased it, "They're as unpredictable as sin. Just when you think that you know what they'll do, they always do the opposite. Never count on them doing what you want."

Never count on them doing what you want. Yet that is exactly what Nate had done. He had counted on Scar making a break for it early on. Now all those warriors and women were dead, and more would die from their wounds. And it was all on his shoulders.

Placing his forearms across his knees, Nate rested his forehead on them. He felt awful, a sickness of the spirit that no herbal balm could soothe. When this was over, he prayed to God he never had to kill another grizzly as long as he lived. Provided he survived, naturally.

Nate had never set out to become the champion grizzly-killer of all time. Had it been up to him, he would have gone his whole life long and never slain a single one. But by some quirk of fate, some outworking of destiny beyond his ken, events conspired to force him into situations where it was kill or be killed. And he liked being alive.

That was ever the way, though, Nate reflected. Fate had a knack for twisting a person's life into knots and adding complications no one wanted. It was as if the puppeteer pulling the strings had a macabre sense of humor, if not an outright cruel streak. Most folks, Nate among them, would rather go from day to day without heartache or hardship. All he asked was to be permitted to live it in peace, surrounded by those he loved most. But peace and love were the exceptions, not the rule.

Nate tended to regard life as a forge in which men and women were tempered by hardship until they were as tough as steel. Some became so inured to the gentler aspects that they lost sight of them completely. In their eyes it was a dog-eat-dog world, and the devil take the hindmost.

Not to Nate. In all his struggles, through all his hardships, he never let himself lose sight of the fundamental values that made live worth living: the love of a good wife and a caring family. They were the true treasures that made all the rest endurable.

Nate felt fingers of drowsiness pluck at him, and lifting his head, he shook it vigorously to fend them off. Time enough to sleep later. For now, he must do his part to help the Utes. Standing, he walked over to Neota, who was overseeing the disposition of the dead and the care of the wounded, and signed, "Question. How can I help?"

Neota smiled and signed, "You have brought an end to Scar. That is help enough."

Nearby, a woman who had been bitten through the shoulder was grimacing and trembling as friends administered to her. Blood caked her neck and splotched her buckskin dress. She had to be in intense anguish, but she did not let out a peep.

"We should not put the travois before the horse." Nate paraphrased the white figure of speech. "We do not know if the bear will die."

"We find out tomorrow, Grizzly Killer," Neota signed. "And if Scar is not dead, he will be by sunset."

Nate let it drop. Since his help wasn't needed, he went to check on his horses. They were picketed near where the chief's lodge had stood. Starting a fire, he occupied himself making coffee. He needed to keep busy. To divert his thought from the carnage. He tried thinking about Winona and Evelyn, but that only made him feel worse. In the act of reaching for his coffee tin, he heard a low cough.

It was Niwot again.

"What do you want?" Nate demanded.

"To talk," the young warrior signed, and without being asked, he sat down cross-legged on the other side of the fire.

"What do we have to talk about?" Nate was in no mood for more of Niwot's nonsense. If the youth brought up marrying Evelyn just one more time, Nate was going to punch him in the mouth.

"We should talk about you. I have watched you closely since the fight. I saw your sign talk with Neota. You blame yourself for so many dying."

Nate stared in unconcealed amazement. Never in a million years would he have suspected Niwot of being so understanding. So mature. "What if I do?"

"You are wrong. My people have lived in terror of Scar for more winters than I have lived. He has killed members of every band. The Kaputa, the Mahagwhch, the Pahwant, the Toompamauach, the Cunumba, the Weeminuche, the Kapota, all had given up hope. Then you came, and brought new hope with you."

Nate opened the tin and carefully poured enough grounds into the strainer to make a suitable pot. He had to ration his coffee or he would run out. When he looked up, Niwot had more to sign.

"You did what no other has done, Grizzly Killer. You inspired us to fight back. All you see now are the bodies and the blood. But when I look at my people, I see the pride in their eyes. Pride that was not there one sleep ago."

"Which would the dead rather have?" Nate asked. "Pride, or their life back?"

Niwot sighed and stood. "Do all white men have rocks between their ears?"

Nate stared at the young warrior's retreating back. He still resented the youth's interest in Evelyn, but he had to admit he didn't feel quite as bad about how his plan had worked out. He lifted the top to place it back on the pot.

Someone else was coming toward him, an old woman with more gray in her hair than black. She walked with a slight stoop to her back, and had to use a cane. "May I talk with you, Grizzly Killer?"

Nate motioned, and she came nearer. "Would you like some coffee?"

"I am Hototo's woman."

Dumbfounded, Nate did not know what to sign. He

couldn't begin to guess what she was doing there.

"My husband was killed by Scar."

"I know. I am sorry. I liked him," Nate told her.

"And he liked you. Last night he said that if all whites were like you, there would never be any trouble between your people and ours."

"That was kind of him." Nate never suspected the old warrior thought so highly of him. "Are you sure you would not like some coffee?"

"No. But I will sit a moment." She carefully lowered herself down, her legs folded under her. "There is something I would like to know. Something Hototo said he would ask you, but now he is gone and I must ask myself."

"I will answer any question you have."

"Why did you kill my son?"

Astounded, Nate responded, "You must have me confused with someone else. I do not know your son."

She did not seem to see his fingers move. "It was almost twenty winters ago. He had gone off with four friends, north toward Shoshone country. Only two came back alive. They said that Carcajou and one other white—you—killed our son and the other two. I would like to know why."

Out of the dim recesses of Nate's past surfaced a memory long forgotten. Of the time his mentor, Shakespeare McNair, decided to take him to his first rendezvous. Called Carcajou by the Indians, McNair had done his level best to avoid trouble when five Utes spotted them.

"You remember now," the old woman signed. It was a statement, not a question.

"I remember. Your son and his friends chased us down and tried to kill us. We had to defend ourselves."

"I thought it must be something like that. My son was always out to count coup. It was all he thought of."

"The two who made it back should have told you how he died."

"They did. But I wanted to hear it from your own lips." Propping her cane under her, she started to rise.

Nate jumped up, gripped her elbow, and helped her the

rest of the way. "I am sorry. Had I to do it again—"

"You would do as you did before. Just as we would dig the pits and build the towers and wait for Scar had we to do it again. There are things that must be done whether we want to do them or not. Life does not always give us a choice. So do not blame yourself for Hototo's death. He died trying to slay the great slayer of our people, and he will long be remembered for his bravery. It is the most any warrior can ask. As for me, my oldest daughter will take me in, but not for long. I expect to die by the next moon. I want to go join Hototo." Smiling sweetly, she hobbled off.

First Niwot, now the old woman. Realizing he hadn't earned her name, Nate took a step to go after her when from out of the vastness of the mountains to the south rumbled a roar of primal fury and bestial defiance.

Scar wasn't done for yet.

Not by a long shot.

Chapter Eleven

Seventeen warriors rode from the village at dawn. More would have gone, but so many had died the night before or were lying in their lodges fighting for life that Neota decided it was all that could be spared. The rest of the able-bodied men had to stay behind in case of an enemy raid. So they, along with most of the women and children, gathered to see Neota and his warriors off.

A somber mood prevailed. Everyone seemed to sense that at long, long last, Scar's end had come. Everyone also realized that Scar would not die alone. The rogue would take as many of them with him as he could. The partings between husbands and wives and fathers and their children were touching and bittersweet.

Nate rode at the head of the hunting party. On his right trotted Neota. On his left, to his considerable surprise, was Niwot. They forded the river at the exact point Scar had and on the far bank found tracks and a copious trail of blood leading into the forest.

"He is hurt to death," Neota signed.

Nate begged to differ. The length of the grizzly's stride proved Scar had been moving at a swift clip. That, despite having upward of forty arrows stuck in his hide and more wounds than there were stars. To say nothing of the pints of blood Scar was losing with every mile he covered. Nate had to marvel at the bear's stamina. And to wonder why it was making a beeline for the high country.

Most wild animals, when gravely stricken, retreated to secluded spots to die in solitude. From the look of things, either Scar wasn't as hurt as they thought, or the spot the grizzly had chosen was far off. Either way, it was soon evident they had a long ride ahead of them, and they paced their mounts accordingly.

The Utes rarely spoke to one another, and when they did it was in low voices. They sat their horses broom-straight, always alert, always ready in case Scar had doubled back and sprang on them from ambush.

By the middle of the day they were well up the mountain. Twisting in his saddle, Nate enjoyed a sweeping vista of the valley and the surrounding peaks. It made him think of his own little valley and filled him with an intense longing to return to where he belonged.

Neota presently called a halt to rest their animals. Nate dismounted and moved about to stretch his legs, and a moment later a short shadow attached itself to his own. "Go talk to someone else, Niwot," he signed.

The youth wore his customary smirk. "Did I hurt your feelings last night, Grizzly Killer? I did not mean to."

"No man, red or white, likes being insulted."

"But every man, red and white, should have a sense of humor. My words were not meant to hurt your feelings."

"Where I come from, saying someone has rocks between their ears is not considered a compliment." Nate had noticed that the rest of the warriors in the hunting party were considerably older, and he took some small measure of pleasure in signing, "Why did Neota let someone your age come along? This is a job for men."

David Thompson

"I asked to join. I told him I could not let anything happen to the father of my future wife."

Nate had tolerated as much as he was going to. "Niwot, I have something to tell you. Pay attention. It is important." Nate stopped signing for a few seconds to draw out the suspense. "My daughter will never marry you."

"Why not?"

"For more reasons than I care to talk about. But the most important one is that she does not like living in the wilderness. She plans to go live in a white village far to the east of the prairie as soon as she is sixteen winters old." Nate smiled. He didn't regret puncturing the youngster's hopes. It served him right for being so cocky.

Niwot absorbed the information, then calmly signed, "I am not worried. She will change her mind."

"You do not know my daughter."

"And you, Grizzly Killer, do not know me." So signing, Niwot walked toward his horse.

Nate's exasperation with the young lunkhead climbed. Niwot's skull had to be thicker than Scar's. What did it take to get through to him? he asked himself. Since he seriously doubted anything would ever come of it, he shrugged and focused on the matter at hand. A scan of the upper slopes turned up no trace of their quarry. Scar had a substantial lead and must be miles ahead. Perhaps even over the range into the next valley. Catching him would take more time than Nate reckoned.

Soon Neota climbed on his paint and everyone followed suit. The tracks took them on up through a broad belt of mixed spruce and firs. Above that was talus, which Scar had traversed but which Neota would not. He was loath to endanger their animals. They had to go around, and the detour cost them.

Nate's stomach growled, but he didn't care. Food could wait. He noticed that the blood trail was lessening and Scar was going faster than before. That bear had to be made of iron; how else to account for him lasting so long?

* * *

Wilderness #40: Scar

The pain was always there. It filled every fiber of his being. In pounding waves it would worsen, taper off, then worsen again. Over and over and over, like storm-tossed waves pounding a lakeshore. Yet even when it slackened it was still the worst agony Scar had ever felt. Worse, even, than the time the Feather Heads hurt him when he tried to stop them from killing his mother.

The pain hammered like the beat of a second heart deep within Scar's head, making it hard for him to think. He was moving on instinct, drawn by an urge he could not define toward the highest slopes. Up there vegetation was scant and other creatures few. But that was where, on another mountain and in another time, Caregiver had her den. The only true home Scar had known. The only place he had ever been happy.

Scar reached the heights when the sun was directly above him. He had been there previously and knew of a broad overlook at the rim of a drop-off. To reach it required using a mountain goat trail barely wide enough for his paws and extremely precarious to any animal larger than a goat. But he had climbed it before, and he would not let the pain stop him from climbing it now.

The ascent taxed Scar to his limit, but finally he stood on the overlook and drank in the view. It seemed as if he could see to the ends of the earth. More tired than he could ever remember being, Scar slowly sank onto his belly. So simple an act, yet it speared agony through his tortured frame. He laid his head on his paws and closed his eyes. He wanted to sleep. He wanted the bliss of slumber to claim him until well past the time of the cold and snow. But the incessant pounding pain wouldn't let him. He tried shifting his huge body to make himself more comfortable, but no position helped. He was too badly hurt.

Feathered sticks jutted from Scar like small limbs from a tree. So many that when he twisted his head and looked back, it seemed he had more feathers than hair. He began tearing out as many as he could reach with his teeth. Some snapped under the pressure, and there was nothing he could do about it except leave the barbed tips embedded in his flesh. He pulled out as many as there were claws in his front paws, but it was nowhere near enough to ease the torment.

With the long sticks Scar fared better. Most were embedded in his front shoulders and sides, and he was able to reach them with his jaws. It took some doing, but he pulled them out, all except for one that transfixed his flank so deep, the tip grated against bone when he moved.

More blood flowed, and Scar could spare little. He had already shed more than he realized he had, enough to fill a pond, and for a time it had left him weaker than a newborn cub.

Scar knew he was going to die. He could not say how he knew that, but he did. He should never have turned on the Feather Heads. The moment they sprang from under those hides, he should have made for the river. But the sight of them, fueled by the sting of the first few feathered sticks, had caused something deep within him to snap. He had wanted to kill and kill and kill until there wasn't a Feather Head left.

Their resistance surprised him. They had fought with a ferocity Scar never saw before. Even the shes. He was accustomed to them fleeing at the sight of him, but these had joined the males in trying to slay him and fought as fiercely as Caregiver or Nice.

Thinking of his sister brought warmth to Scar's chilled veins. He always wanted to see her again after that day at the river. He hoped she was alive somewhere, raising more cubs of her own as Caregiver had raised them.

A terrible ache in Scar's hindquarters prompted him to shift position again, onto his side. He heard the crack of Feather Sticks breaking and several stabbing pangs from their sharp barbs. Remembering how sick they made him after the fight to save Caregiver, he knew he should find water. But he lacked the energy to rise.

The sun felt good on Scar's battered body. He would have been content to lie there indefinitely had a vagrant gust of wind not brought him a troubling scent from below. Sluggishly lifting his head, he scanned the lower slopes. He did not spot them right away. They were far down the mountain yet, winding upward through dense woodland.

Feather Heads.

A low growl rumbled from Scar's chest. He should have known they would not let him be. They were as determined to end his life as he was to end theirs. Resting his chin on the edge, he watched them climb. It would take them a long while yet to reach the goat trail. He could move on long before they arrived. Go over the mountain and lose them in the rugged country to the south. His other option was to wait. To rest and gather his strength, and when the right time came, to kill as many of them as he could before they finished what they had started all those many summers ago.

It was really no choice at all. Scar ran last night, but he would not run now. Let them come. They must think him severely hurt, and he was, but when they reached the top they would learn just how much fight was left in him.

An uneasy feeling came over Nate King. A feeling they were being spied on. Ahead was a sawtooth ridge sprinkled by boulders. Look though he did, he saw nothing to account for his feeling. Not that he needed confirmation. There was only one explanation. Kneeing the bay up alongside Neota, he signed, "Scar is not far off."

"Let us hope so. My wife and daughters cry out for his blood."

Them, or Neota? Nate mused. The Ute leader had pushed hard all day, unrelenting in his drive to end it once and for all. The warriors were tired, their mounts showing signs of fatigue after almost ten solid hours of continuous climbing.

Scar had stopped bleeding long ago, but his tracks were plain as day. It puzzled Nate that Scar made no attempt whatsoever to shake off possible pursuers. The lack of caution was out of character and further proof the grizzly must be mortally wounded.

The ground leveled at the base of a ridge, and Neota reined up. Swiveling, he addressed the other warriors in his own tongue and then addressed Nate in sign. "We will rest our horses a short while."

Nate squinted at the sun, which was well on its westward arc. They had three hours of daylight, possibly a bit more. Were it up to him, they would make camp for the night and not move on until dawn. For the horses, if for no other reason. But there was one. If he was right about Scar being up there, they could be riding right into trouble.

To Nate's annoyance, Niwot approached. He couldn't understand why the young warrior didn't take the hint and leave him be. "What now?" he signed.

"I would like to know why."

Stepping to a knee-high boulder, Nate took a seat. "Why fish live in water and we do not? Why fire is hot and ice is cold? Why some people cannot help being rude all the time?" His sarcasm was lost on the other.

"No. I would like to know why Blue Flower plans to go live with whites in the land beyond the prairie."

"Were your eyes shut when I told you? She does not like wilderness life."

"Why not? What have you done to turn her against it?"

"Me?" Nate signed sharply. "I had nothing to do with it. She made the decision on her own."

"You are her parent. You set the example by which she lives. If she does not like living here, then you have done or said something to make her think it is not for her."

Out loud, in English, Nate muttered, "What I wouldn't give to be able to chuck you off this mountain." In sign he said, "I raised my daughter to make up her own mind about things. I am the one who likes it here, remember? Her decision to leave has nothing to do with me." Nate gazed at several adjacent peaks mantled in ivory. "If it did, she would never go."

Niwot wasn't done. "Is it true all whites live in lodges made of wood?"

"Except for those who live in lodes made of stone, yes."

"Lodges that stand in one place, and cannot be moved as ours can?"

Wilderness #40: Scar

"Some white lodges weigh as much as all the lodges in your village combined. Who would want to move them?"

"Is it true many whites do not cook their own game but have others do it for them? That they do not know how to cure hides or sew their own clothes, either?"

"Those who live in what you would call large villages, yes. But those who live in the wild still fend for themselves." Nate became curious. "Where did you learn all this?"

"When I went with Neota to your lodge. While you were sick in bed your woman told us much about white ways. She claimed many whites do not know how to hunt or fish."

"She spoke with a straight tongue," Nate conceded.

"Then most of your people are lazy and stupid. Why your daughter would want to live among them I cannot understand."

"Do not judge all of us by the acts of some."

"I could never live in a white village. Perhaps I should visit Blue Flower and make her see it would be a mistake."

"There are white customs you should be aware of before you come see her," Nate noted. "Customs I expect suitors to honor."

"I will do my best to do so, Grizzly Killer. What are they?"

"The first and most important is that no suitor can visit my daughter without my consent."

"Do I have it?"

"No."

Niwot grinned as if he thought Nate was joking, then scowled when it hit him that Nate was finished signing. Fidgeting nervously, he asked, "You truly do not want me to court your daughter?"

"I told you before. By white custom she is much too young."

"And I told you before. I am willing to wait three or four winters. Then I will visit whether you want me to or not."

Nate mentally counted to twenty. By then the youth was over talking to several warriors. He saw Neota studying the crest and walked over. "How do you intend to reach the top?" Much of the face was too steep.

Neota indicated a ribbon of a trail to the east that looped upward in a series of tight switchbacks.

"That might be fine for mountain goats, but not for horses."

"Ours can make it," Neota signed confidently. "We will take turns so we are spaced well apart. Should one fall, it will not take any others with it."

"Why not wait until morning and find a better way? If Scar is hurt as bad as you believe, he might be dead by then." Which would suit Nate just fine. Better they find the griz dead than lose more Utes. But Neota didn't see it that way.

"If he is not dead, he will be that much farther away by morning. We must catch him now while we can."

The warriors mounted and made for the game trail. Nate was second in line, behind Neota and in front of Niwot, who for some strange reason persisted in sticking close to him. Nate saw goat tracks and a few mule deer prints, and then, defined in loose dirt, one of Scar's paw prints. Calling out Neota's name, he drew rein and pointed.

"I saw," the Ute leader signed, and grimly smiled. "We are close. Very close."

Nate was convinced more than ever that the grizzly was waiting for them. At some point between the base of the ridge and the top, Scar would tear into them like a rabid wolf. "Let me go first," he signed.

"Why you?" Neota asked.

Nate patted his Hawken. "My rifle has a better chance of bringing Scar down than your arrows or your lance."

"It did not bring Scar down last night." Neota rode on.

Frowning, Nate followed. His friend seemed to have conveniently forgotten that his rifle had brought down the other grizzly. And he would do the same to Scar, if only he could get a clear shot.

The climb was precarious. Often there was barely enough space for a horse to put one hoof in front of the other.

Wilderness #40: Scar

Neota's mount frequently balked and had to be goaded into going higher. Just below the rim, Neota reined up. He was waiting, Nate suspected, to try and lure the grizzly into showing itself. But Scar never appeared, and after a couple of minutes Neota finished the last leg of the climb. After riding up and over, he dismounted and waved to tell them all was clear.

Then it was Nate's turn. The bay gave him no problems, principally because Nate had ridden it over trails like this before. He kept glancing back and forth between the trail and the rim for sign of Scar. Suddenly, while negotiating the third switchback, one of the bay's front hooves slipped on loose stones. The horse stumbled, and they started to go over the side. Several Utes cried out. Nate hauled on the reins with all his strength, and the bay regained its footing, then went on as if nothing had happened.

Nate's heart had been in his throat. It was sobering to realize the same could happen to any of them, at any time. The last switchback was the narrowest yet, but the bay made it around safely. Thankfully, a little farther on, the trail widened enough for them to easily gain the summit.

Neota was scouring the ground for tracks. "Scar rested here awhile," he signed, "but has moved on."

The overlook afforded a spectacular vista, but Nate was in no frame of mind to appreciate it. He scanned the escarpment for sign of Scar. Scrub brush and boulders covered a roughly rectangular area about seventy yards long and half that wide. None of the boulders were large enough to conceal a goat, let alone a grizzly. Nor was the brush all that heavy.

Swinging off the bay, Nate walked to the overlook, The impression of a heavy body showed where Scar had lain for the longest time watching them, but a short while ago the bear had risen and headed to the south. Nate dogged the huge bruin's tracks until he came to an alpine slope on the other side of the ridge. The tracks led down it into thick timber.

Satisfied, Nate returned to await the rest of the hunting

party. Niwot and a handful of warriors were in earnest conversation with Neota, and it appeared an argument was brewing. Nate could guess why. Neota was all for pushing on, but some of the others would rather make camp.

Nate didn't become involved. It would do no good. Neota had his mind made up and there was no changing it. Which was unfortunate for the horses. Most were lathered with sweat, and so tired their heads drooped.

While waiting, Nate returned to the overlook. The feathered ends of seven broken arrows were scattered about, and sprinkled among them were drops of dry blood. Scar had to be in pain so severe it defied the imagination. How the bear kept going was beyond him. Sinking onto a knee, Nate picked up a broken shaft and inspected it for more blood. There was very little. The likelihood of Scar bleeding to death was slim.

An unwanted shadow crossed his, and Niwot stepped in front of him. "What would you like to do, Grizzly Killer?" he signed. "Some of us want to go on. Some want to stop here. Others want to go back."

Nate pushed to his feet. The last of the Utes had reached the summit and dismounted, and three separate groups had formed. Heated exchanges were taking place, and from their expressions, no one was willing to back down.

"I think we should stop for the night," Niwot signed. "But I will do what you do. No harm must come to the father of my future wife."

"Stop signing that." Some people, Nate reflected, just never learned. "When my daughter agrees to be your wife, then you can say it." Which would happen when buffalo sprouted wings. "Until then, call me Grizzly Killer and nothing but Grizzly Killer."

Neota was angrily upbraiding the others. He was in the wrong, but he couldn't see it. Their animals needed rest, water, and grass or they would be of no use come morning.

Nate was going to stress that fact but was distracted by the sixteen-year-old thorn in his side.

"I have heard that some whites have two names, a white

name and an Indian name. What is your white name?"

"Now is hardly the time."

"They will argue awhile yet. And I would very much like to know."

Nate told him.

Like a child forming its first words, Niwot repeated the name, trying to pronounce it right. "Ny-ate Ky-ng. Ny-ate Ky-ng."

"Close enough. But you can still call me Grizzly Killer."

Only two warriors were ready to ride on with Neota. The rest hung back as he moved to his warhorse and gripped the mane.

"Wait," Nate signed, and hurried over. He thought it would rid him of Niwot, but the youth was glued to his side. "You cannot avenge Star At Morning and your daughters if you are dead, Neota."

"Are you staying behind too, my friend? I thought you were the one I could count on the most."

"I am," Nate signed. Come what may, he would never desert him. "So listen to me when I tell you to do as most of the others want and make camp. Not for them, for the horses. Look at yours and tell me I am wrong."

Neota's mouth pinched tight. "They are exhausted. I know. But they will last until sunset. Then they will have all night to recover."

"Would you push so hard if it were a bear other than Scar? Would you ride your horse into the ground to catch a wolf or a mountain lion?"

"He killed my family!" Neota signed, his throat bobbing. Overcome by emotion, he leaned against his horse and cupped his hands over his face.

Nate waited for the chief to compose himself. If he could calm Neota down and persuade him to use some common sense, he could prevent a rift that would deplete their numbers. They needed every warrior they had.

"We should let him be," Niwot signed.

Nate stayed put. He was about to explain to the youth the importance of sticking together when Niwot's eyes widened to the size of walnuts and he took several halting steps backward. Niwot was gazing past him, toward the boulders and the scrub brush. His gut churning, Nate whirled.

Twenty-five yards to the east, an immense form was rising up out of a hollow no one had suspected was there. The rest of Utes were so busy arguing, they hadn't noticed.

Voicing a roar that shook the peaks, Scar lowered his huge head and charged.

Chapter Twelve

Nate King was rooted in shock for all of three seconds. Not much time, but enough for Scar to cover more than half the distance to the Utes. Snapping the Hawken to his shoulder, he took a swift bead while shouting, "Look out!" None of the warriors spoke a lick of English, but he thought the cry would give them a few moments' forewarning. Instead, much to his dismay, they turned toward him to see what he was yelling about, putting their backs to the onrushing grizzly.

Niwot frantically started yelling, but by then it was too late.

Nate fired a hair's-width before Scar slammed into the Utes. He couldn't tell if it had any effect, because the rogue ripped into them like a scythe into grass. Five or six were down before the rest galvanized to life. Lances were hoisted and arrows notched to bow strings, but they were so close together most couldn't employ their weapons for fear of hitting their friends.

Reloading as he ran, Nate sprinted to the right. He had

to get broadside to the bear. A heart shot was their only hope.

Suddenly a new element entered the mix. The Utes had left their horses unattended. Now, panicked, some bolted off across the ridge. Others whinnied and reared, their flailing hooves posing an additional peril. Still others galloped to the mountain goat trail to try and escape, but they were moving much too fast. Nate saw two go tumbling over the edge in a whirl of limbs, mane, and tail, and lost sight of them as they pitched down the slope.

Nine of the seventeen Utes were down, dead or dying. Arrows began to fly as those still alive spread out and fought back. Others thrust their lances into Scar's neck, sides, and flanks.

In a blur Scar spun and caught an unsuspecting Ute across the face with a forepaw. There was a sickening splat of flesh, the crunch of bone, and the warrior's lifeless body hit the ground with a spine-shattering *crack*.

Several more arrows pierced the grizzly's hide. A lance sheared deep under his front shoulder. Scar swiveled to pounce on another Ute but was thwarted by an unexpected source.

One of the warhorses turned on him. A superb roan, its neck painted with symbols that betokened its prowess in battle, had risen onto its hind legs and was windmilling its front hooves at Scar's head and face. The grizzly had to back away or have his skull caved in. He swiped at the horse but missed, then pivoted to one side as the roan's forelegs came slamming down to earth.

Again the warhorse reared, driving the great bear back.

Four of the seven remaining Utes unleashed arrows as rapidly as their fingers allowed. The other three had hurled lances and were dashing to the bodies of fallen companions to gather up others.

Nate was almost ready. He only needed another few seconds. But in a fight for life, where every instant was an eternity, that was long enough for all sorts of unforeseen things to happen, and it did.

With a sweep of his blood-drenched claws, Scar disemboweled the warhorse. As the animal pitched on its side and its intestines spilled onto the ground, Scar darted at an Ute about to throw a lance. One blow, and the man's rib cage was reduced to splinters.

Only six Utes were left, among them Neota and Niwot. The youth was shoulder to shoulder with the others, firing shaft after shaft. As he reached over his shoulder for another, Scar bounded toward him. A paw rose to administer a death stroke.

Nate had the Hawken reloaded. He was standing less than ten feet from the griz, and slightly behind it. Sighting squarely on where the beast's heart should be, he fired.

Scar's tree-trunk legs buckled and he pitched headlong to the ground, momentum carrying him to within inches of Niwot. Yelping, the youth leaped back.

The rest of the Utes were frozen in amazement. They thought Scar was dead, but Nate wasn't so sure, and drew one of his pistols. Grizzlies were too remarkably tenacious of life to assume anything.

Relief and joy rippled across Niwot's features, and he yipped in cheerful abandon. Several of the other Utes smiled.

But they were premature. For the next second Scar heaved up off the ground and did the last thing Nate reckoned he would do: He ran. Wheeling, Scar barreled toward the south side of the ridge.

Nate extended his arm to fire, but shooting the bear in the hind end would be pointless, and he lowered it again.

Screeching like a cougar, Netoa bounded in pursuit. The rest of the Utes were a step behind, howling in feral chorus. Niwot hesitated, but only a few seconds. Then he, too, joined the mad rush to finish the bear off.

"No! Wait!" Nate shouted. They weren't thinking straight. They had no hope of catching Scar before he reached the heavy timber on the south slope. The wise thing to do was collect their mounts, then go after him. They could hold their own a lot better on horseback than they could on foot.

Nate's bay was one of the few horses that had not run off. Running over, he shoved the pistol under his belt, snagged the reins, and forked leather. As he trotted toward the south rim he commenced to reload the Hawken. His heavy-caliber pistols could bring down an elk at short range, but for sheer killing power they couldn't compare to the Hawken.

It was as Nate feared. The Utes had reached the top of the south slope, but Scar was already disappearing into the trees. They scampered down it like so many coyotes, throwing caution to the wind in their rash eagerness to catch up to him.

Reloading while riding wasn't a feat everyone could perform. Nate had to exercise care not to spill any black powder, and when it came time to tamp the ball down, he had to guide the bay with his legs rather than the reins to free both hands. As he entered the forest he glimpsed the Utes bounding to the southwest like so many antelope. They were following a fresh blood trail. Scar was bleeding again, and bleeding badly. It was only a matter of time before the Utes cornered him.

Or was it the other way around? Nate wouldn't put it past Scar to double back and take them from behind. The bear had displayed an uncanny knack for striking when the Utes were least apt to expect it. Circling around and hiding in the hollow had been a stroke of bestial brilliance. Once again Nate was impressed by the bear's intelligence. It was almost humanlike in its breadth and complexity.

Nate had come to believe there was something fundamentally different about Scar. Something that set him apart from other grizzlies. Maybe Scar had been born smarter than most, although that alone wouldn't explain Scar's decades-long vendetta against the Utes.

Bears weren't renowned for long memories. Yet Nate had a suspicion that Scar remembered the death of his mother all those many years ago. It had to be the missing piece of the puzzle in the bear's otherwise inexplicable behavior.

The other night, Nate had wondered if Scar might be a throwback to an earlier era. Shoshone legend, substantiated by the legends of other tribes, had it that at one time the mountains and the plains were overrun by animals much different from those that lived there now. Giants, many of them. Strange creatures three times the size of buffalo, with horns growing from the sides of their mouths. Long-necked creatures able to graze the tops of trees. Enormous cats with teeth as long as a man's arm. Birds with wingspans longer than the tallest lodgepole. And bears of such size and ferocity, they were the most feared of all.

When Nate was younger, he had taken the legends with a large grain of salt. But as he grew older and saw with his own eyes sights no other white man had ever seen, he came to accept the legends as containing more fact than fancy.

It was possible, then, that Scar was a bear born out of his rightful time. That he should have lived ages ago when his kind were lords of the earth.

Yet regardless, Scar had to die.

Nate rested the Hawken's stock on his left leg but kept his thumb on the hammer and his finger on the trigger. The Utes had slowed and were fanning out. He couldn't see the griz anywhere, but they must think they were getting close.

Here in the timber the shadows were lengthening as the day drew to a close, cloaking the woods in an early twilight. Nate had to remind himself that the gloom could play tricks with a man's eyes and make him think he was seeing things that weren't there. Such as a particularly large shadow with an uncanny resemblance to the silhouette of a bear. But it was only a shadow, nothing more.

Suddenly the undergrowth to Nate's right rustled. Something was moving through it on a course that would bring it uncomfortably close to the bay. He saw brownish fur and slapped the Hawken to his shoulder.

The brush parted, and out stepped a familiar shape. It was staring at the Utes, not at him. Hearing the bay, though, the animals turned, snorted, and fled, its tail rising like a flag. It was a buck, and nothing more.

The Utes had stopped, and Neota was signing for the others to converge on a spot up ahead.

Nate still hadn't spotted Scar. He nearly jumped out of his buckskins when a twig snapped to his left and another large animal burst through a thicket. It flashed in front of the bay, then went bounding off after the buck. It had been a doe, nothing more.

Grinning to himself, Nate lowered the Hawken. He had to steady his nerves. He was much too jumpy. It could well be that the grizzly was a mile off by now.

Then a colossal monstrosity towered up out of nowhere, and a high-pitched screech was ripped from the throat of a Ute warrior whose body folded like an accordion when an immensely powerful paw came crashing down on the crown of his head. Before the other Utes could retaliate, the grizzly spun and vanished into the undergrowth.

Nate spurred the bay over to the latest victim. He knew there was nothing any of them could do, which proved to be an understatement. It looked as if a ten-ton boulder had fallen on the warrior's head. His body had crumpled in on itself, and the legs were little better than stumps. Broken bones bristled through ruptured skin and buckskin like pins from a pincushion, a sight Nate had seen much too frequently of late.

Neota and the other four Utes were staring at the grisly pile that just seconds earlier had been a living, breathing human being, their emotions ranging from rage to revulsion.

One of the warriors made a comment and was answered by several others. Niwot leaned his bow against his chest to sign to Nate, "Why do you think Scar ran off like that, Grizzly Killer? Why did he not attack the rest of us?"

Nate couldn't say. So few of them were left, by rights the grizzly should have kept swinging and biting until they were all down. More of that unpredictable bear behavior, he reckoned. "Let me go in front," he signed, and did so to nip any objections in the bud.

Scar had left a swath of crushed vegetation a five-year-old could follow. It wasn't like him. The grizzly had to be up to something, but exactly what remained to be seen. Nate rode with the Hawken cocked and tucked to his shoulder. No sounds disturbed the unnatural silence except the clomp of the bay's hooves.

Suddenly the swath ended, and there was no sign of the bear's passage whatsoever. No tracks. No bent grass. It lent the impression that Scar had vanished into thin air. Since that was preposterous, Nate leaned to either side, seeking to find the direction Scar had gone.

One of the Utes yelled. A roar drowned it out, and Nate swiveled in time to see that the grizzly had circled back and reared up out of a thicket that didn't appear big enough to hide a cougar, let along a creature his size. Scar's forepaws slashed twice, and the Ute who had yelled fell with his chest ripped to ribbons.

The others rushed Scar. Neota hurled his lance. Niwot and another warrior loosed arrows. And just as Scar turned to pull his vanishing act again, Nate centered his rifle on the bear's neck and stroked the trigger.

The boom of the thunder stick was simultaneous with a jarring blow that rocked Scar's head. It spiked new pain through his tortured body but did not stop him from wheeling and loping well out of the two-legs' sight. Halting, he nearly collapsed, overcome once again by the dizziness that had been afflicting him since the fight on the ridge. The bouts came and went, each worse than the last.

Scar's vision clouded, and the world around him spun like a whirlpool in a river. His stomach churned. His ears rang. He heard a hissing sound that he could not identify, and the spattering of what sounded like raindrops.

At length the spinning ceased and Scar's senses were restored. He twisted his head toward the hissing and saw that the leaves and boles of nearby trees and bushes were sprinkled with scarlet drops. Blood was spraying from the new wound in his neck, just as he had seen it do many times from animals and Feather Heads he had slain.

Wood Eater Head was to blame. Wood Eater Head and the thunder stick. Scar had been concentrating on the Feather Heads, since they were the ones he hated most. But if he was to finish off the rest before his own end came, he must first deal with the hairy two-leg.

Scar sensed he was running out of time. From deep within his being had risen an almost overpowering urge to go off into the heart of the forest to be by himself. But he suppressed it. He refused to die just yet.

Scar began to circle back around, as he had done before. The Feather Heads were doing exactly as he wanted. They had let themselves be drawn into the forest, where they were always so easy to slay, and now were blundering after him in their typically clumsy fashion. He could hear them even though they tried to move stealthily, and lifting his nose, he pinpointed exactly where they were.

Scar stopped circling and padded toward the sound of Wood Eater Head's Mane. Only a few more to kill and he could go off to end his days in peace. He had not slain all the Feather Heads there were, as he once intended, but he had made them pay dearly for what they did to his mother.

The Mane was near. Scar slowed and crouched, his belly scraping the ground as he crept along until he could see Wood Eater Head, and behind him, now bunched close together, the Feather Heads. They had learned from the fate of the other two.

Scar tensed his body. Soon the black Mane would be abreast of where he was hidden. A short sprint, and he would bowl it over and dispose of Wood Eater Head before Wood Eater Head could use the thunder stick. He dug his claws into the ground and girded himself for his rush.

Nate's mouth was so dry, he had to swallow twice to moisten it. Every nerve was jangling; the griz could come roaring out of the undergrowth at any second. He would only have time for one shot, and then only if he spotted the bear before it reached him. He thought he saw something off among the pines, the outline of a hump starting to rise, but when he peered closer, it wasn't there.

The Utes were only a few steps behind. Moving shoulder-to-shoulder, each warrior faced in a different direction so the rouge couldn't get at them without being seen.

The bay nickered and looked off toward the spot where Nate thought he had glimpsed a hump. They had passed it and Nate twisted around, thinking the griz had been there all along. But there was nothing, nothing at all.

Where was Scar?

The dizziness again. The roiling of his stomach. Scar had started to rise to launch himself at his enemies when another wave of weakness struck him and he had to sink onto the ground, as helpless as a day-old bobcat. It was the worst attack yet. He thought that maybe this was the end. That his desire to kill these final few two-legs would go unfulfilled.

Gradually, though, the vertigo and the churning faded, leaving Scar with a bitter taste in his mouth and a burning sensation in his chest. Wood Eater Head and the Utes had gone on by. Slowing rising, he watched until they were out of sight. Two of the Feather Heads had been walking backward and would have spotted him if he emerged sooner.

Scar shadowed them. The hissing had stopped, but he was terribly light-headed. He could collapse at any moment.

Images of Caregiver and his siblings filtered through Scar's mind. Of his mother affectionately nuzzling him. Of snuggling against her for warmth in cold weather. Of wrestling Mean and Nice. How he missed those times. How he wished they had never ended.

More dizziness struck him, but it wasn't quite severe enough to bring Scar to a stop. The contents of his stomach tried to come back up; he swallowed them down. He must act, and act now, or it would be too late.

* * *

"Where is he?" Neota signed when Nate glanced back. "Why does he wait?"

Nate had been wondering the same thing. The horizon was swallowing the sun, and soon it would be dark. They would be lucky if they spotted the grizzly before he was breathing down their necks. Maybe that was the reason Scar was holding off. Maybe Scar was waiting for night to fall so he would have the advantage.

A clearing opened before them. Drawing rein in the center, Nate turned the bay sideways so Scar could not reach the Utes from that side without going through him.

"Why did you stop?" Neota inquired.

"We should make a stand," Nate proposed. And here was as good a spot as any, with eight to ten feet of open space between them and the trees.

The Utes looked at one another. Neota directed a few comments at Niwot and motioned for the youth to move closer to the bay, but Niwot answered harshly and stayed where he was.

That was when the bay's ears rose and the big black gazed northward, back the way they had come. Nate probed the gathering darkness but saw nothing that would account for it. One of the Utes suddenly took a step in the same direction, tilted his head, and said something that caused the others to stiffen and raise their weapons.

Then Nate heard what the Ute had heard: the distant crack and snap of undergrowth. It grew rapidly louder. Something was barreling toward them like a mad bull, plowing through everything in its path. From the racket it sounded like a herd of stampeding buffalo.

Nate raised his Hawken.

Tree limbs were breaking with retorts like gunshots. Brush splintered and popped like fireworks. The crackling swiftly swelled to a crescendo, and under it all beat the increasingly heavy thud of ponderous paws.

Off in the darkness a moving mountain appeared, hurtling toward them with the speed of a fur-covered comet. A pair of blazing coals were fixed unblinkingly on the clearing, and on those in it. Nearer and nearer they came, as louder and louder rose the din.

The bay chose that moment to nicker and took a prancing step to one side. Nate glanced down to make sure that the horse wasn't about to run off, and when he glanced up again, there was Scar, hurtling out of the dark and across the clearing, his bulk seeming to blot out half the forest. Two barbed shafts flew to meet him. Neota and another warrior hurled their lances. But they might as well have thrown pebbles.

Nate rushed his shot. The grizzly was almost to the Utes when he squeezed the trigger. He couldn't have missed at that range, but Scar didn't break stride. At full speed the bear slammed into Neota and the others, scattering them like chaff in a gale. Nate grabbed for a pistol but couldn't clear his belt before Scar slammed into the bay with the impact of a battering ram.

A high-pitched squeal rang in Nate's ears as the horse was smashed out from under him. He was upended and smacked down on his left shoulder hard enough to jar the breath from his lungs. He heard the bay squeal again, and fearful the grizzly had it down, he shoved up onto his knees and drew both flintlocks.

The bay was on its side, struggling to rise, easy prey for Scar, but the grizzly wasn't after the horse. Scar wanted the Utes. Niwot and another were on the ground, too dazed to stand. Neota was on one knee. The fourth man had stood but was shaking his head to clear it. He didn't see the grizzly surge onto its hind legs, didn't see the huge arms that enfolded him in an unbreakable hug.

Nate levered to his feet and ran to the right for a clear shot. As he raised a pistol, Neota leaped between them, onto the bear's broad back. Clinging with one arm to the hump, Neota buried his gleaming knife again and again.

The warrior in Scar's clutches fought desperately to break free, but his hands were empty and the best he could do was rain ineffective punches on Scar's bloodstained neck and disfigured face. A snap of Scar's razor teeth severed one of his arms at the wrist. A second bite tore half his neck away. He sagged, the life fading fast from his eyes, as Scar flung him aside and turned toward Niwot and the other warrior still on the ground.

Neota let go of the bear's hump and darted around to stab Scar in the chest. He was much too close. A backward sweep of Scar's forepaw catapulted him head over heels into a pine tree.

Nate aimed at Scar's right ear and fired. The grizzly staggered but still would not fall. The third Ute picked that moment to stand and send two arrows, swift as thought, into Scar's ribs. Roaring ferociously, Scar lunged and closed his jaws on the warrior's head. The outcome was as horrendous as it was final.

Scar dropped onto all fours and turned toward Niwot. The youth was on his knees, nocking an arrow. Scar had only two steps to take to reach him, but Nate got there first. Jamming the second flintlock against Scar's hairless cheek, Nate thumbed back the hammer and squeezed the trigger. He never saw the blow that lifted him off his feet.

For a few seconds Nate lay stunned, but only for a few. He looked up to see Scar lumber toward him. Niwot had darted out of reach and was letting fly with shaft after shaft, trying to stop the bear from reaching him. He had lost the Hawken and both pistols, but he still had his Bowie and his tomahawk, and unlimbering both, he rose into a crouch.

Part of Scar's face was missing, and blood was pouring from his new wounds in a torrent. Indestructible, unstoppable, he rose onto his back legs.

Nate sprang, arcing the tomahawk high and thrusting the Bowie low. Both sliced deep, and he ducked under a paw that nearly took his head off. Skipping to one side, he sank the Bowie in to the hilt. Fetid breath assailed him and he ducked a second time. Above him, Scar's teeth gnashed on empty air.

Nate leaped back and set himself for the bear's next rush. It was slower than before, so slow that Nate sidestepped it and drove the tomahawk into Scar's head, behind the ear. A claw nicked his buckskin shirt.

Scar roared, or tried to, then swayed like a tree cut off at the roots. Nate dived to the right as the rogue crashed to earth, narrowly missing him. Straightening, he raised the tomahawk but checked his swing. There was no need.

The scourge of the central Rockies was dead.

Neota limped out of the trees, a knot on his forehead the size of a goose egg. "It is over," he wearily signed. "Truly, finally over."

"The last of the great ones," Nate said aloud, He surprised the two Utes, and himself, by kneeling and placing a hand on what was left of Scar's head. "There will never be another like him."

"That is good," Neota signed. "One was more than enough. My people will honor you for generations."

Nate felt no joy, no elation. Instead, a peculiar sadness came over him. Shaking it off with a toss of his head, he began collecting his guns. The bay was across the clearing, upright and unhurt.

Niwot came over, carrying a pistol.

"Thank you." Nate had to admit that the youth had performed bravely and might not be the complete dunderhead he had branded him as. But he should have known better.

"When we reach the village, Grizzly Killer, I would like to talk to you about your daughter—"

WILDERNESS

Fang & Claw
David Thompson

To survive in the untamed wilderness a man needs all the friends he can get. No one can battle the continual dangers on his own. Even a fearless frontiersman like Nate King needs help now and then and he's always ready to give it when it's needed. So when an elderly Shoshone warrior comes to Nate asking for help, Nate agrees to lend a hand. The old warrior knows he doesn't have long to live and he wants to die in the remote canyon where his true love was killed many years before, slain by a giant bear straight out of Shoshone myth. No Shoshone will dare accompany the old warrior, so he and Nate will brave the dreaded canyon alone. And as Nate soon learns the hard way, some legends are far better left undisturbed.

___4862-0 $3.99 US/$4.99 CAN

Dorchester Publishing Co., Inc.
P.O. Box 6640
Wayne, PA 19087-8640

Please add $2.50 for shipping and handling for the first book and $.75 for each book thereafter. NY, NYC, and PA residents, please add appropriate sales tax. No cash, stamps, or C.O.D.s. All orders shipped within 6 weeks via postal service book rate. Canadian orders require $2.50 extra postage and must be paid in U.S. dollars through a U.S. banking facility.

Name_____
Address_____
City_____State_____Zip_____
I have enclosed $ _____ in payment for the checked book(s).
Payment <u>must</u> accompany all orders. ❑ Please send a free catalog.
CHECK OUT OUR WEBSITE! www.dorchesterpub.com

WILDERNESS

#28
The Quest
David Thompson

Life in the brutal wilderness of the Rockies is never easy. Danger can appear from any direction. Whether it's in the form of hostile Indians, fierce animals, or the unforgiving elements, death can surprise any unwary frontiersman. That's why Nate King and his family have mastered the fine art of survival—and learned to provide help to their friends whenever necessary. So when one of Nate's neighbors shows up at his cabin more dead than alive, frantic with worry because his wife and child had been taken by Indians, Nate doesn't hesitate for a second. He knows what he has to do—he'll find his friend's family and bring them back safely. Or die trying.

___4572-9 $3.99 US/$4.99 CAN

WILDERNESS

Mountain Nightmare

David Thompson

Frontiersmen are drawn to the wilderness of the Rockies by the quest for freedom, but in exchange for this precious liberty they must endure a life of constant danger. Nate King and his family have faced every vicious predator in the mountains, both human and animal, and triumphed. But what of a predator that is neither human nor animal…or a little of both? Nate and his neighbors have begun to find tracks and other signs of a being the Shoshones know as one of the Old Ones, a half-man, half-beast creature that preys on humans and kills simply for the sake of killing. Can the old legends really be true? And if they are, how can even the best hunter on the frontier survive becoming the hunted?

___4656-3 $3.99 US/$4.99 CAN

WILDERNESS

BLOOD FEUD

<————————————————————>

David Thompson

The brutal wilderness of the Rocky Mountains can be deadly to those unaccustomed to its dangers. So when a clan of travelers from the hill country back East arrive at Nate King's part of the mountain, Nate is more than willing to lend a hand and show them some hospitality. He has no way of knowing that this clan is used to fighting—and killing—for what they want. And they want Nate's land for their own!

___4477-3 $3.99 US/$4.99 CAN

KIT CARSON
BLOOD RENDEZVOUS
DOUG HAWKINS

The high point of any trapper's year is the summer rendezvous, the annual gathering where mountain men from all over the frontier meet to trade the pelts they risked their lives for. But for Kit Carson, the real danger lies in getting to the rendezvous. He is leading a party of trappers, all of them weighed down with a year's worth of furs. That is enough to make them a tempting target for any killer on the trail—especially when the trail leads through Blackfoot territory.

_4499-4 $3.99 US/$4.99 CAN

Dorchester Publishing Co., Inc.
P.O. Box 6640
Wayne, PA 19087-8640

Please add $1.75 for shipping and handling for the first book and $.50 for each book thereafter. NY, NYC, and PA residents please add appropriate sales tax. No cash, stamps, or C.O.D.s. All orders shipped within 6 weeks via postal service book rate.
Canadian orders require $2.00 extra postage and must be paid in U.S. dollars through a U.S. banking facility.

Name_____
Address_____
City_____State_____Zip_____
I have enclosed $_____ in payment for the checked book(s).
Payment <u>must</u> accompany all orders. ❑ Please send a free catalog.
CHECK OUT OUR WEBSITE! www.dorchesterpub.com

WILD BILL
DEAD MAN'S HAND
JUDD COLE

Marshal, gunfighter, stage driver, and scout, Wild Bill Hickok has a legend as big and untamed as the West itself. No man is as good with a gun as Wild Bill, and few men use one as often. From Abilene to Deadwood, his name is known by all—and feared by many. That's why he is hired by Allan Pinkerton's new detective agency to protect an eccentric inventor on a train ride through the worst badlands of the West. With hired thugs out to kill him and angry Sioux out for his scalp, Bill knows he has his work cut out for him. But even if he survives that, he has a still worse danger to face— a jealous Calamity Jane.

___4487-0 $3.99 US/$4.99 CAN

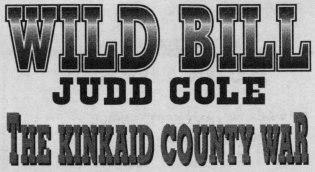

WILD BILL

JUDD COLE

THE KINKAID COUNTY WAR

Wild Bill Hickok is a legend in his own lifetime. Wherever he goes his reputation with a gun precedes him—along with an open bounty of $10,000 for his arrest. But Wild Bill is working for the law when he goes to Kinkaid County, Wyoming. Hundreds of prime longhorn cattle have been poisoned, and Bill is sent by the Pinkerton Agency to get to the bottom of it. He doesn't expect to land smack dab in the middle of an all-out range war, but that's exactly what happens. With the powerful Cattleman's Association on one side and land-grant settlers on the other, Wild Bill knows that before this is over he'll be testing his gun skills to the limit if he hopes to get out alive.

___4529-X $3.99 US/$4.99 CAN

Dorchester Publishing Co., Inc.
P.O. Box 6640
Wayne, PA 19087-8640

Please add $1.75 for shipping and handling for the first book and $.50 for each book thereafter. NY, NYC, and PA residents, please add appropriate sales tax. No cash, stamps, or C.O.D.s. All orders shipped within 6 weeks via postal service book rate. Canadian orders require $2.00 extra postage and must be paid in U.S. dollars through a U.S. banking facility.

Name_____
Address_____
City_____ State_____ Zip_____
I have enclosed $_____ in payment for the checked book(s).
Payment <u>must</u> accompany all orders. ❑ Please send a free catalog.
    CHECK OUT OUR WEBSITE! www.dorchesterpub.com